The Blacker the Berry

Wallace Thurman

The blacker the berry
The sweeter the juice . . .
        —*Negro folk saying*

My color shrouds me in . . .
        —*Countee Cullen*

Part 1

Emma Lou

More acutely than ever before Emma Lou began to feel that her luscious black complexion was somewhat of a liability, and that her marked color variation from the other people in her environment was a decided curse. Not that she minded being black, being a Negro necessitated having a colored skin, but she did mind being too black. She couldn't understand why such should be the case, couldn't comprehend the cruelty of the natal attenders who had allowed her to be dipped, as it were, in indigo ink when there were so many more pleasing colors on nature's palette. Biologically, it wasn't necessary either; her mother was quite fair, so was her mother's mother, and her mother's brother, and her mother's brother's son; but then none of them had had a black man for a father. Why *had* her mother married a black man? Surely there had been some eligible brown-skin men around. She didn't particularly desire to have had a "high yaller" father, but for her sake certainly some more happy medium could have been found.

She wasn't the only person who regretted her darkness either. It was an acquired family characteristic, this moaning and grieving over the color of her skin. Everything possible had been done to alleviate the unhappy condition, every suggested agent had been employed, but her skin, despite bleachings, scourgings, and powderings, had remained black—fast black—as nature had planned and effected.

She should have been a boy, then color of skin wouldn't have

1

mattered so much, for wasn't her mother always saying that a black boy could get along, but that a black girl would never know anything but sorrow and disappointment? But she wasn't a boy; she was a girl, and color did matter, mattered so much that she would rather have missed receiving her high school diploma than have to sit as she now sat, the only odd and conspicuous figure on the auditorium platform of the Boise high school. Why had she allowed them to place her in the center of the first row, and why had they insisted upon her dressing entirely in white so that surrounded as she was by similarly attired pale-faced fellow graduates she resembled, not at all remotely, that comic picture her Uncle Joe had hung in his bedroom? The picture wherein the black, kinky head of a little red-lipped pickaninny lay like a fly in a pan of milk amid a white expanse of bedclothes.

But of course she couldn't have worn blue or black when the call was for the wearing of white, even if white was not complementary to her complexion. She would have been odd-looking anyway no matter what she wore and she would also have been conspicuous, for not only was she the only dark-skinned person on the platform, she was also the only Negro pupil in the entire school, and had been for the past four years. Well, thank goodness, the principal would soon be through with his monotonous farewell address, and she and the other members of her class would advance to the platform center as their names were called and receive the documents which would signify their unconditional release from public school.

As she thought of these things, Emma Lou glanced at those who sat to the right and to the left of her. She envied them their obvious elation, yet felt a strange sense of superiority because of her immunity for the moment from an ephemeral mob emotion. Get a diploma?—What did it mean to her? College?—Perhaps. A job?—Perhaps again. She was going to have a high school diploma, but it would mean nothing to her whatsoever. The tragedy of her life was that she was too black. Her face and not a slender roll of ribbon-bound parchment was to be her future identification tag in society. High school diploma indeed! What she needed was an efficient bleaching agent, a magic cream that would remove this unwelcome black mask from her face and make her more like her fellow men.

"Emma Lou Morgan."

She came to with a start. The principal had called her name and stood smiling down at her benevolently. Some one—she knew it was her Cousin Buddie, stupid imp—applauded, very faintly, very provokingly. Some one else snickered.

"Emma Lou Morgan."

The principal had called her name again, more sharply than before and his smile was less benevolent. The girl who sat to the left of her nudged her. There was nothing else for her to do but to get out of that anchoring chair and march forward to receive her diploma. But why did the people in the audience have to stare so? Didn't they all know that Emma Lou Morgan was Boise high school's only nigger student? Didn't they all know—but what was the use. She had to go get that diploma, so summoning her most insouciant manner, she advanced to the platform center, brought every muscle of her lithe limbs into play, haughtily extended her shiny black arm to receive the proffered diploma, bowed a chilly thanks, then holding her arms stiffly at her sides, insolently returned to her seat in that foreboding white line, insolently returned once more to splotch its pale purity and to mock it with her dark, outlandish difference.

Emma Lou had been born in a semi-white world, totally surrounded by an all-white one, and those few dark elements that had forced their way in had either been shooed away or else greeted with derisive laughter. It was the custom always of those with whom she came into most frequent contact to ridicule or revile any black person or object. A black cat was a harbinger of bad luck, black crepe was the insignia of mourning, and black people were either evil niggers with poisonous blue gums or else typical vaudeville darkies. It seemed as if the people in her world never went halfway in their recognition or reception of things black, for these things seemed always to call forth only the most extreme emotional reactions. They never provoked mere smiles or mere melancholy, rather they were the signal either for boisterous guffaws or pain-induced and tear-attended grief.

Emma Lou had been becoming increasingly aware of this for a long time, but her immature mind had never completely grasped its full, and to her tragic, significance. First there had been the case of her father, old black Jim Morgan they called him, and Emma Lou had often wondered why it was that he of all the people she heard discussed by her family should always be referred to as if his very blackness condemned him to receive no respect from his fellow men.

She had also begun to wonder if it was because of his blackness that he had never been in evidence as far as she knew. Inquiries netted very unsatisfactory answers. "Your father is no good." "He left your mother, deserted her shortly after you were born." And these statements were always prefixed or followed by some epithet such as "dirty black no-gooder" or "durn his onery black hide." There was in fact only one member of the family who did not speak of her father in this manner, and that was her Uncle Joe, who was also the only person in the family to whom she really felt akin, because he alone never seemed to regret, to bemoan, or to ridicule her blackness of skin. It was her grandmother who did all the regretting, her mother who did the bemoaning, her Cousin Buddie and her playmates, both white and colored, who did the ridiculing.

Emma Lou's maternal grandparents, Samuel and Maria Lightfoot, were both mulatto products of slave-day promiscuity between male masters and female chattel. Neither had been slaves, their own parents having been granted their freedom because of their close connections with the white branch of the family tree. These freedmen had migrated into Kansas with their children, and when these children had grown up they in turn had joined the westward-ho parade of that current era, and finally settled in Boise, Idaho.

Samuel and Maria, like many others of their kind and antecedents, had had only one compelling desire, which motivated their every activity and dictated their every thought. They wished to put as much physical and mental space between them and the former home of their parents as was possible. That was why they had left Kansas, for in Kansas there were too many reminders of that which their parents had escaped and from which they wished to flee. Kansas was too near the former slave belt, too accessible to disgruntled southerners, who, deprived of their slaves, were inculcated with an easily communicable virus, nigger hatred. Then, too, in Kansas all Negroes were considered as belonging to one class. It didn't matter if you and your parents had been freedmen before the Emancipation Proclamation, nor did it matter that you were almost three-quarters white. You were, nevertheless, classed with those hordes of hungry, ragged, ignorant black folk arriving from the South in such great numbers, packed like so many stampeding cattle in dirty, manure-littered box cars.

From all of this these maternal grandparents of Emma Lou fled, fled to the Rocky Mountain states which were too far away for the recently freed slaves to reach, especially since most of them believed that the world ended just a few miles north of the Mason-Dixon line. Then, too, not only were the Rocky Mountain states beyond the reach of this raucous and smelly rabble of recently freed cotton pickers and plantation hands, but they were also peopled by pioneers, sturdy land and gold seekers from the East, marching westward, always westward in search of El Dorado, and being too busy in this respect to be violently aroused by problems of race unless economic factors precipitated matters.

So Samuel and Maria went into the fast farness of a little known Rocky Mountain territory and settled in Boise, at the time nothing more than a trading station for the Indians and whites, and a red light center for the cowboys and sheepherders and miners in the neighboring vicinity. Samuel went into the saloon business and grew prosperous. Maria raised a family and began to mother nuclear elements for a future select Negro social group.

There was of course in such a small and haphazardly populated community some social intermixture between whites and blacks. White and black gamblers rolled the dice together, played tricks on one another while dealing faro, and became allies in their attempts to outfigure the roulette wheel. White and black men amicably frequented the saloons and dancehalls together. White and black women leaned out of the doorways and windows of the jerry-built frame houses and log cabins of "Whore Row." White and black housewives gossiped over back fences and lent one another needed household commodities. But there was little social intercourse on a higher scale. Sluefoot Sal, the most popular high yaller on "Whore Row," might be a buddy to Irish Peg and Blond Liz, but Mrs. Amos James, whose husband owned the town's only dry-goods store, could certainly not become too familiar with Mrs. Samuel Lightfoot, colored, whose husband owned a saloon. And it was not a matter of the difference in their respective husbands' businesses. Mrs. Amos James did associate with Mrs. Arthur Emory, white, whose husband also owned a saloon. It was purely a matter of color.

Emma Lou's grandmother then, holding herself aloof from the inmates of "Whore Row," and not wishing to associate with such as old Mammy Lewis' daughters, who did most of the town wash, and others of their ilk, was forced to choose her social equals slowly and carefully. This was hard, for there were so few Negroes in Boise anyway that there wasn't much cream to skim off. But as the years passed, others, who, like Maria and her husband, were mulatto offsprings of mulatto freedmen seeking a freer land, moved in, and were soon initiated into what was later to be known as the blue vein circle, so named because all of its members were fair-skinned enough for their blood to be seen pulsing purple through the veins of their wrists.

Emma Lou's grandmother was the founder and the acknowledged leader of Boise's blue veins, and she guarded its exclusiveness passionately and jealously. Were they not a superior class? Were they not a very high type of Negro, comparable to the persons of color groups in the West Indies? And were they not entitled, ipso facto, to more respect and opportunity and social acceptance than the more pure blooded Negroes? In their veins was some of the best blood of the South. They were closely akin to the only true aristocrats in the United States. Even the slave masters had been aware of and acknowledged in some measure their superiority. Having some of Marse George's blood in their veins set them apart from ordinary Negroes at

birth. These mulattoes as a rule were not ordered to work in the
fields beneath the broiling sun at the urge of a Simon Legree
lash. They were saved and trained for the more gentle jobs,
saved and trained to be ladies' maids and butlers. Therefore, let
them continue this natural division of Negro society. Let them
also guard against unwelcome and degenerating encroach-
ments. Their motto must be "Whiter and whiter every generation," until the grandchildren of the blue veins could easily go
over into the white race and become assimilated so that problems of race would plague them no more.

Maria had preached this doctrine to her two children, Jane
and Joe, throughout their apprentice years, and can therefore
be forgiven for having a physical collapse when they both, first
Joe, then Emma Lou's mother, married not mulattoes, but a
copper brown and a blue black. This had been somewhat of a
necessity, for, when the mating call had made itself heard to
them, there had been no eligible blue veins around. Most of
their youthful companions had been sent away to school or else
to seek careers in the eastern cities, and those few who had
remained had already found their chosen life's companions.
Maria had sensed that something of the kind might happen and
urged Samuel to send Jane and Joe away to some eastern boarding school, but Samuel had very stubbornly refused. He had his
own notions of the sort of things one's children learned in
boarding school, and of the greater opportunities they had to
apply that learning. True, they might acquire the same knowledge in the public schools of Boise, but then there would be
some limit to the extent to which they could apply this knowledge, seeing they lived at home and perforce must submit to
some parental supervision. A cot in the attic at home was to
Samuel a much safer place for a growing child to sleep than an
iron four poster in a boarding school dormitory.

So Samuel had remained adamant and the two carefully
reared scions of Boise's first blue vein family had of necessity
sought their mates among the lower orders. However, Joe's wife
was not as undesirable as Emma Lou's father, for she was almost
three-quarters Indian, and there was scant possibility that her
children would have revolting dark skins, thick lips, spreading

nostrils, and kinky hair. But in the case of Emma Lou's father there were no such extenuating characteristics, for his physical properties undeniably stamped him as a full-blooded Negro. In fact, it seemed as if he had come from one of the few families originally from Africa, who could not boast of having been seduced by some member of southern aristocracy, or befriended by some member of a strolling band of Indians.

No one could understand why Emma Lou's mother had married Jim Morgan, least of all Jane herself. In fact she hadn't thought much about it until Emma Lou had been born. She had first met Jim at a church picnic, given in a woodlawn meadow on the outskirts of the city, and almost before she had realized what was happening she had found herself slipping away from home, night after night, to stroll down a well-shaded street, known as Lover's Lane, with the man her mother had forbidden her to see. And it hadn't been long before they had decided that an elopement would be the only thing to assure themselves the pleasure of being together without worrying Mama Lightfoot's wrath, talkative neighbors, prying town marshals, and grass stains.

Despite the rancor of her mother and the whispering of her mother's friends, Jane hadn't really found anything to regret in her choice of a husband until Emma Lou had been born. Then all the fears her mother had instilled in her about the penalties inflicted by society upon black Negroes, especially upon black Negro girls, came to the fore. She was abysmally stunned by the color of her child, for she had been certain that since she herself was so fair that her child could not possibly be as dark as its father. She had been certain that it would be a luscious admixture, a golden brown with all its mother's desirable facial features and its mother's hair. But she hadn't reckoned with nature's perversity, nor had she taken under consideration the inescapable fact that some of her ancestors, too, had been black and that some of their color chromosomes were still imbedded within her. Emma Lou had been fortunate enough to have hair like her mother's, a thick, curly black mass of hair, rich and easily controlled, but she had also been unfortunate enough to have a face as black as her father's, and a nose which, while not exactly flat, was as distinctly negroid as her too thick lips.

Her birth had served no good purpose. It had driven her mother back to seek the confidence and aid of Maria, and it had given Maria the chance she had been seeking to break up the undesirable union of her daughter with what she termed an ordinary black nigger. But Jim's departure hadn't solved matters at all, rather it had complicated them, for although he was gone, his child remained, a tragic mistake which could not be stamped out or eradicated even after Jane, by getting a divorce from Jim and marrying a red-haired Irish Negro, had been accepted back into blue vein grace.

Emma Lou had always been the alien member of the family and of the family's social circle. Her grandmother, now a widow, made her feel it. Her mother made her feel it. And her Cousin Buddie made her feel it, to say nothing of the way she was regarded by outsiders. As early as she could remember, people had been saying to her mother, "What an extraordinary black child! Where did you adopt it?" or else, "Such lovely unnigger-ish hair on such a niggerish-looking child." Some had even been facetious and made suggestions like, "Try some lye, Jane, it may eat it out. She can't look any worse."

Then her mother's re-marriage had brought another person into her life, a person destined to give her, while still a young child, much pain and unhappiness. Aloysius McNamara was his name. He was the bastard son of an Irish politician and a Negro washerwoman, and until he had been sent East to a parochial school, Aloysius, so named because that was his father's middle name, had always been known as Aloysius Washington, and the identity of his own father had never been revealed to him by his proud and humble mother. But since his father had been pre-vailed upon to pay for his education, Aloysius' mother thought it the proper time to tell her son his true origin and to let him assume his real name. She had hopes that away from his home town he might be able to pass for white and march unhindered by bars of color to fame and fortune.

But such was not to be the case, for Emma Lou's prospective stepfather was so conscious of the Negro blood in his veins and so bitter because of it, that he used up whatever talents he had groaning inwardly at capricious fate, and planning revenge upon the world at large, especially the black world. For it was Negroes and not whites whom he blamed for his own, to him, life's tragedy. He was not fair enough of skin, despite his mother's and his own hopes, to pass for white. There was a brownness in his skin, inherited from his mother, which immediately marked him out for what he was, despite the red hair and the Irish blue eyes. And his facial features had been modeled too generously. He was not thin lipped, nor were his nostrils as delicately chiseled as they might have been. He was a Negro. There was no getting around it, although he tried every possible way to do so.

Finishing school, he had returned West for the express purpose of making his father accept him publicly and personally advance his career. He had wanted to be a lawyer and figured that his father's political pull was sufficiently strong to draw him beyond race barriers and set him as one apart. His father had not been entirely cold to these plans and proposals, but his father's wife had been. She didn't mind her husband giving this nigger bastard some of his money, and receiving him in his home on rare and private occasions. She was trying to be liberal, but she wasn't going to have people point and say, "That's Boss McNamara's wife. Wonder if that nigger son is his'n or hers. They do say. . . ." So Aloysius had found himself shunted back into the black world he so despised. He couldn't be made to realize that being a Negro did not necessarily indicate that one must also be a ne'er-do-well. Had he been white, or so he said, he would have been a successful criminal lawyer, but being considered black it was impossible for him ever to be anything more advanced than a Pullman car porter or a dining car waiter, and acting upon this premise, he hadn't tried anything else.

His only satisfaction in life was the pleasure he derived from insulting and ignoring the real blacks. Persons of color, mulattoes, were all right, but he couldn't stand detestable black Negroes. Unfortunately, Emma Lou fell into this latter class, and suffered at his hands accordingly, until he finally ran away from his wife, Emma Lou, Boise, Negroes, and all, and ran away to Canada with Diamond Lil of "Whore Row."

Summer vacation was nearly over and it had not yet been

decided what to do with Emma Lou now that she had graduated from high school. She herself gave no help nor offered any suggestions. As it was, she really did not care what became of her. After all it didn't seem to matter. There was no place in the world for a girl as black as she anyway. Her grandmother had assured her that she would never find a husband worth a dime, and her mother had said again and again, "Oh, if you had only been a boy!" until Emma Lou had often wondered why it was that people were not able to effect a change of sex or at least a change of complexion.

It was her Uncle Joe who finally prevailed upon her mother to send her to the University of Southern California in Los Angeles. There, he reasoned, she would find a larger and more intelligent social circle. In a city the size of Los Angeles there were Negroes of every class, color, and social position. Let Emma Lou go there where she would not be as far away from home as if she were to go to some eastern college.

Jane and Maria, while not agreeing entirely with what Joe said, were nevertheless glad that at last something which seemed adequate and sensible could be done for Emma Lou. She was to take the four year college course, receive a bachelor degree in education, then go South to teach. That, they thought, was a promising future, and for once in the eighteen years of Emma Lou's life every one was satisfied in some measure. Even Emma Lou grew elated over the prospects of the trip. Her Uncle Joe's insistence upon the differences of social contacts in larger cities intrigued her. Perhaps he was right after all in continually reasserting to them that as long as one was a Negro, one's specific color had little to do with one's life. Salvation depended upon the individual. And he also told Emma Lou, during one of their usual private talks, that it was only in small cities one encountered stupid color prejudice such as she had encountered among the blue vein circle in her home town.

"People in large cities," he had said, "are broad. They do not have time to think of petty things. The people in Boise are fifty years behind the times, but you will find that Los Angeles is one of the world's greatest and most modern cities, and you will be happy there."

On arriving in Los Angeles, Emma Lou was so busy observing the colored inhabitants that she had little time to pay attention to other things. Palm trees and wild geraniums were pleasant to behold, and such strange phenomena as pepper trees and century plants had to be admired. They were very obvious and they were also strange and beautiful, but they impinged upon only a small corner of Emma Lou's consciousness. She was minutely aware of them, necessarily took them in while passing, viewing the totality without pondering over or lingering to praise their stylistic details. They were, in this instance, exquisite theatrical props, rendered insignificant by a more strange and a more beautiful human pageant. For Emma Lou, who, in all her life, had never seen over five hundred Negroes, the spectacle presented by a community containing over fifty thousand, was sufficient to make relatively commonplace many more important and charming things than the far famed natural scenery of Southern California.

She had arrived in Los Angeles a week before registration day at the university, and had spent her time in being shown and seeing the city. But whenever these sightseeing excursions took her away from the sections where Negroes lived, she immediately lost all interest in what she was being shown. The Pacific Ocean itself did not cause her heartbeat to quicken, nor did the roaring of its waves find an emotional echo within her. But on coming upon Bruce's Beach for colored people near Redondo, or the little strip of sandied shore they had appropriated for themselves at Santa Monica, the Pacific Ocean became an intriguing something to contemplate as a background for their activities. Everything was interesting as it was patronized, reflected through, or acquired by Negroes.

Her Uncle Joe had been right. Here, in the colored social circles of Los Angeles, Emma Lou was certain that she would find many suitable companions, intelligent, broad-minded people of all complexions, intermixing and being too occupied otherwise to worry about either their own skin color or the skin color of those around them. Her Uncle Joe had said that Negroes were Negroes whether they happened to be yellow, brown, or black, and a conscious effort to eliminate the darker elements would neither prove nor solve anything. There was nothing quite so silly as the creed of the blue veins: "Whiter and whiter, every generation. The nearer white you are the more white people will respect you. Therefore all light Negroes marry light Negroes. Continue to do so generation after generation, and eventually white people will accept this racially bastard aristocracy, thus enabling those Negroes who really matter to escape the social and economic inferiority of the American Negro."

Such had been the credo of her grandmother and of her mother and of their small circle of friends in Boise. But Boise was a provincial town, given to the molding of provincial people with provincial minds. Boise was a backward town out of the mainstream of modern thought and progress. Its people were cramped and narrow, their intellectual concepts stereotyped and static. Los Angeles was a happy contrast in all respects.

On registration day, Emma Lou rushed out to the campus of the University of Southern California one hour before the registrar's office was scheduled to open. She spent the time roaming around, familiarizing herself with the layout of the campus and learning the names of the various buildings, some old and vineclad, others new and shiny in the sun, and watching the crowds of laughing students, rushing to and fro, greeting one another and talking over their plans for the coming school year. But her main reason for such an early arrival on the campus had been to find some fellow Negro students. She had heard that there were to be quite a number enrolled, but in her hour's stroll she saw not one, and finally disheartened she got into the line stretched out in front of the registrar's office, and, for the moment, became engrossed in becoming a college freshman.

All the while, though, she kept searching for a colored face, but it was not until she had been duly signed up as a student and sent in search of her advisor that she saw one. Then three colored girls had sauntered into the room where she was having a conference with her advisor, sauntered in, arms interlocked, greeted her advisor, then sauntered out again. Emma Lou had wanted to rush after them——to introduce herself, but of course

it had been impossible under the circumstances. She had immediately taken a liking to all three, each of whom was what is
known in the parlance of the black belt as high brown, with
modishly shingled bobbed hair and well-formed bodies, fash-
ionably attired in flashy sport garments. From then on Emma
Lou paid little attention to the business of choosing subjects and
class hours, so little attention in fact that the advisor thought her
exceptionally tractable and somewhat dumb. But she liked students to come that way. It made the task of being advisor easy.
One just made out the program to suit oneself, and had no
tedious explanations to make as to why the student could not
have such and such a subject at such and such an hour, and why
such and such a professor's class was already full.

After her program had been made out, Emma Lou was
directed to the bursar's office to pay her fees. While going down
the stairs she almost bumped into two dark-brown-skinned
boys, obviously brothers if not twins, arguing as to where they
should go next. One insisted that they should go back to the
registrar's office. The other was being equally insistent that they
should go to the gymnasium and make an appointment for their
required physical examination. Emma Lou boldly stopped when
she saw them, hoping they would speak, but they merely glanced
up at her and continued their argument, bringing cards and
pamphlets out of their pockets for reference and guidance.
Emma Lou wanted to introduce herself to them, but she was
too bashful to do so. She wasn't yet used to going to school with
other Negro students, and she wasn't exactly certain how one
went about becoming acquainted. But she finally decided that
she had better let the advances come from the others, especially if they were men. There was nothing forward about her,
and since she was a stranger it was no more than right that the
old-timers should make her welcome. Still, if these had been
girls . . . , but they weren't, so she continued her way down the
stairs.

In the bursar's office, she was somewhat overjoyed at first to
find that she had fallen into line behind another colored girl
who had turned around immediately, and, after saying hello,
announced in a loud, harsh voice:

"My feet are sure some tired!"

Emma Lou was so taken aback that she couldn't answer. People in college didn't talk that way. But meanwhile the girl was continuing:

"Ain't this registration a mess?"

Two white girls who had fallen into line behind Emma Lou snickered. Emma Lou answered by shaking her head. The girl continued:

"I've been standin' in line and clumbin' stairs and talkin' and a-singin' till I'm just 'bout done for."

"It is tiresome," Emma Lou returned softly, hoping the girl would take a hint and lower her own strident voice. But she didn't.

"Tiresome ain't no name for it," she declared more loudly than ever before, then, "Is you a new student?"

"I am," answered Emma Lou, putting much emphasis on the "I am."

She wanted the white people who were listening to know that she knew her grammar if this other person didn't. "Is you," indeed! If this girl was a specimen of the Negro students with whom she was to associate, she most certainly did not want to meet another one. But it couldn't be possible that all of them—those three girls and those two boys for instance—were like this girl. Emma Lou was unable to imagine how such a person had ever gotten out of high school. Where on earth could she have gone to high school? Surely not in the North. Then she must be a southerner. That's what she was, a southerner—Emma Lou curled her lips a little—no wonder the colored people in Boise spoke as they did about southern Negroes and wished that they would stay South. Imagine any one preparing to enter college saying "Is you," and, to make it worse, right before all these white people, these staring white people, so eager and ready to laugh. Emma Lou's face burned.

"Two mo', then I goes in my sock."

Emma Lou was almost at the place where she was ready to take even this statement literally, and was on the verge of leaving the line. Supposing this creature did "go in her sock!" God forbid!

"Wonder where all the spades keep themselves? I ain't seen but two 'sides you."

"I really do not know," Emma Lou returned precisely and chillily. She had no intentions of becoming friendly with this sort of person. Why she would be ashamed even to be seen on the street with her, dressed as she was in a red-striped sport suit, a white hat, and white shoes and stockings. Didn't she know that black people had to be careful about the colors they affected?

The girl had finally reached the bursar's window and was paying her fees, and loudly differing with the cashier about the total amount due.

"I tell you it ain't that much," she shouted through the window bars. "I figured it up myself before I left home."

The cashier obligingly turned to her adding machine and once more obtained the same total. When shown this, the girl merely grinned, examined the list closely, and said:

"I'm gonna pay it, but I still think you're wrong."

Finally she moved away from the window, but not before she had turned to Emma Lou and said,

"You're next," and then proceeded to wait until Emma Lou had finished.

Emma Lou vainly sought some way to escape, but was unable to do so, and had no choice but to walk with the girl to the registrar's office where they had their cards stamped in return for the bursar's receipt. This done, they went onto the campus together. Hazel Mason was the girl's name. Emma Lou had fully expected it to be either Hyacinth or Geranium. Hazel was from Texas, Prairie Valley, Texas, and she told Emma Lou that her father, having become quite wealthy when oil had been found on his farm lands, had been enabled to realize two life ambitions—obtain a Packard touring car and send his only daughter to a "fust-class" white school.

Emma Lou had planned to loiter around the campus. She was still eager to become acquainted with the colored members of the student body, and this encounter with the crass and vulgar Hazel Mason had only made her the more eager. She resented being approached by any one so flagrantly inferior, any one so noticeably a typical southern darky, who had no business

obtruding into the more refined scheme of things. Emma Lou
planned to lose her unwelcome companion somewhere on campus so that she could continue unhindered her quest for agreeable acquaintances.

But Hazel was as anxious to meet one as was Emma Lou, and
having found her was not going to let her get away without a
struggle. She, too, was new to this environment and in a way was
more lonely and eager for the companionship of her own kind
than Emma Lou, for never before had she come into such close
contact with so many whites. Her life had been spent only
among Negroes. Her fellow pupils and teachers in school had
always been colored, and as she confessed to Emma Lou, she
couldn't get used to "all these white folks."

"Honey, I was just achin' to see a black face," she had said,
and, though Emma Lou was experiencing the same ache, she
found herself unable to sympathize with the other girl, for
Emma Lou had classified Hazel as a barbarian who had most
certainly not come from a family of best people. No doubt her
mother had been a washerwoman. No doubt she had innumer-
able relatives and friends all as ignorant and as ugly as she.
There was no sense in any one having a face as ugly as Hazel's,
and Emma Lou thanked her stars that though she was black, her
skin was not rough and pimply, nor was her hair kinky, nor were
her nostrils completely flattened out until they seemed to
spread all over her face. No wonder people were prejudiced
against dark-skin people when they were so ugly, so haphazard
in their dress, and so boisterously mannered as was this present
specimen. She herself was black, but nevertheless she had come
from a good family, and she could easily take her place in a society of the right sort of people.

The two strolled along the lawn-bordered gravel path which
led to a vine-covered building at the end of the campus. Hazel
never ceased talking. She kept shouting at Emma Lou, shouting
all sorts of personal intimacies as if she were desirous of the
whole world hearing them. There was no necessity for her to
talk so loudly, no necessity for her to afford every one on the
crowded campus the chance to stare and laugh at them as they
passed. Emma Lou had never before been so humiliated and so

embarrassed. She felt that she must get away from her offensive companion. What did she care if she had to hurt her feelings to do so. The more insulting she could be now, the less friendly she would have to be in the future.

"Good-bye," she said abruptly, "I must go home." With which she turned away and walked rapidly in the opposite direction. She had only gone a few steps when she was aware of the fact that the girl was following her. She quickened her pace, but the girl caught up with her and grabbing hold of Emma Lou's arm, shouted,

"Whoa there, Sally."

It seemed to Emma Lou as if every one on the campus was viewing and enjoying this minstrel-like performance. Angrily she tried to jerk away, but the girl held fast.

"Gal, you sure walk fast. I'm going your way. Come on, let me drive you home in my buggy."

And still holding on to Emma Lou's arm, she led the way to the side street where the students parked their cars. Emma Lou was powerless to resist. The girl didn't give her a chance, for she held tight, then immediately resumed the monologue which Emma Lou's attempted leave-taking had interrupted. They reached the street, Hazel still talking loudly, and making elaborate gestures with her free hand.

"Here we are," she shouted, and releasing Emma Lou's arm, salaamed before a sport model Stutz roadster. "Oscar," she continued, "meet the new girl friend. Pleased to meetcha, says he. Climb aboard."

And Emma Lou had climbed aboard, perplexed, chagrined, thoroughly angry, and disgusted. What was this little black fool doing with a Stutz roadster? And of course, it would be painted red—Negroes always bedecked themselves and their belongings in ridiculously unbecoming colors and ornaments. It seemed to be a part of their primitive heritage which they did not seem to have sense enough to forget and deny. Black girl— white hat—red-and-white-striped sport suit—white shoes and stockings—red roadster. The picture was complete. All Hazel needed to complete her circus-like appearance, thought Emma Lou, was to have some purple feathers stuck in her hat.

Still talking, the girl unlocked and proceeded to start the car. As she was backing it out of the narrow parking space, Emma Lou heard a chorus of semi-suppressed giggles from a neighboring automobile. In her anger she had failed to notice that there were people parked in the car next to the Stutz. But as Hazel expertly swung her machine around, Emma Lou caught a glimpse of them. They were all colored and they were all staring at her and Hazel. She thought she recognized one of the girls as being one of the group she had seen earlier that morning, and she did recognize the two brothers she had passed on the stairs. And as the roadster sped away, their laughter echoed in her ears, although she hadn't actually heard it. But she had seen the strain in their faces, and she knew that as soon as she and Hazel were out of sight, they would give free rein to their suppressed mirth.

Although Emma Lou had finished registering, she returned to the university campus on the following morning in order to continue her quest for collegiate companions without the alarming and unwelcome presence of Hazel Mason. She didn't know whether to be sorry for the girl and try to help her or to be disgusted and avoid her. She didn't want to be intimately associated with any such vulgar person. It would damage her own position, cause her to be classified with some one who was in a class by herself, for Emma Lou was certain that there was not, and could not be, any one else in the university just like Hazel. But despite her vulgarity, the girl was not all bad. Her good nature was infectious, and Emma Lou had surmised from her monologue on the day before how utterly unselfish a person she could be and was. All of her store of the world's goods were at hand to be used and enjoyed by her friends. There was not, as she had said, "a selfish bone in her body." But even that did not alter the disgusting fact that she was not one who would be welcome by the "right sort of people." Her flamboyant style of dress, her loud voice, her raucous laughter, and her flagrant disregard or ignorance of English grammar seemed inexcusable to Emma Lou, who was unable to understand how such a person could stray so far from the environment in which she rightfully belonged to enter a first-class university. Now Hazel,

according to Emma Lou, was the type of Negro who should go
to a Negro college. There were plenty of them in the South
whose standard of scholarship was not beyond her ability. And,
then, in one of those schools, her darky-like clownishness would
not have to be paraded in front of white people, thereby causing
discomfort and embarrassment to others of her race, more civilized and circumspect than she.

The problem irritated Emma Lou. She didn't see why it had
to be. She had looked forward so anxiously, and so happily to her
introductory days on the campus, and now her first experience
with one of her fellow colored students had been an unpleasant
one. But she didn't intend to let that make her unhappy. She
was determined to return to the campus alone, seek out other
companions, see whether they accepted or ignored the offend-
ing Hazel, and govern herself accordingly.

It was early and there were few people on the campus. The
grass was still wet from a heavy overnight dew, and the sun had
not yet dispelled the coolness of the early morning. Emma Lou's
dress was of thin material and she shivered as she walked or
stood in the shade. She had no school business to attend to;
there was nothing for her to do but to walk aimlessly about the
campus.

In another hour, Emma Lou was pleased to see that the campus walks were becoming crowded, and that the side streets
surrounding the campus were now heavy with student traffic.
Things were beginning to awaken. Emma Lou became jubilant
and walked with jaunty step from path to path, from building to
building. It then occurred to her that she had been told that
there were more Negro students enrolled in the School of
Pharmacy than in any other department of the university, so,
finding the Pharmacy building, she began to wander through its
crowded hallways.

Almost immediately, she saw a group of five Negro students,
three boys and two girls, standing near a water fountain. She was
both excited and perplexed, excited over the fact that she was so
close to those she wished to find, and perplexed because she did
not know how to approach them. Had there been only one person standing there, the matter would have been comparatively

easy. She could have approached with a smile and said, "Good morning." The person would have returned her greeting, and it would then have been a simple matter to get acquainted.

But five people in one bunch all known to one another and all chatting intimately together!—it would seem too much like an intrusion to go bursting in to their gathering—too forward and too vulgar. Then, there was nothing she could say after having said "good morning." One just didn't break into a group of five and say, "I'm Emma Lou Morgan, a new student, and I want to make friends with you." No, she couldn't do that. She would just smile as she passed, smile graciously and friendly. They would know that she was a stranger, and her smile would assure them that she was anxious to make friends, anxious to become a welcome addition to their group.

One of the group of five had sighted Emma Lou as soon as she had sighted them:

"Who's this?" queried Helen Wheaton, a senior in the College of Law.

"Some new 'pick,' I guess," answered Bob Armstrong, who was Helen's fiancé and a senior in the School of Architecture.

"I bet she's going to take Pharmacy," whispered Amos Blaine.

"She's hottentot enough to take something." mumbled Tommy Brown. "Thank God, she won't be in any of our classes, eh Amos?"

Emma Lou was almost abreast of them now. They lowered their voices, and made a pretense of mumbled conversation among themselves. Only Verne Davis looked directly at her and it was she alone who returned Emma Lou's smile.

"Whatcha grinnin' at?" Bob chided Verne as Emma Lou passed out of earshot.

"At the little frosh, of course. She grinned at me. I couldn't stare at her without returning it."

"I don't see how anybody could even look at her without grinning."

"Oh, she's not so bad," said Verne.

"Well, she's bad enough."

"That makes two of them."

"Two of what, Amos?"

"Hottentots, Bob."

"Good grief," exclaimed Tommy, "why don't you recruit some good-looking co-eds out here?"

"We don't choose them," Helen returned.

"I'm going out to the Southern Branch where the sight of my fellow female students won't give me dyspepsia."

"Ta-ta, Amos," said Verne, "and you needn't bother to sit in my car any more if you think us so terrible." She and Helen walked away, leaving the boys to discuss the sad days which had fallen upon the campus.

Emma Lou, of course, knew nothing of all this. She had gone her way rejoicing. One of the students had noticed her, had returned her smile. This getting acquainted was going to be an easy matter after all. It was just necessary that she exercise a little patience. One couldn't expect people to fall all over one without some preliminary advances. True, she was a stranger, but she would show them in good time that she was worthy of their attention, that she was a good fellow and a well-bred individual quite prepared to be accepted by the best people.

She strolled out onto the campus again trying to find more prospective acquaintances. The sun was warm now, the grass dry, and the campus overcrowded. There was an infectious germ of youth and gladness abroad to which Emma Lou could not remain immune. Already she was certain that she felt the presence of that vague something known as "college spirit." It seemed to enter into her, to make her jubilant and set her very nerves tingling. This was no time for sobriety. It was the time for youth's blood to run hot, the time for love and sport and wholesome fun.

Then Emma Lou saw a solitary Negro girl seated on a stone bench. It did not take her a second to decide what to do. Here was her chance. She would make friends with this girl and should she happen to be a new student, they could become friends and together find their way into the inner circle of those colored students who really mattered.

Emma Lou was essentially a snob. She had absorbed this trait from the very people who had sought to exclude her from their presence. All of her life she had heard talk of the "right sort of people," and of "the people who really mattered," and from these phrases she had formed a mental image of those to whom they applied. Hazel Mason most certainly could not be included in either of these categories. Hazel was just a vulgar little nigger from down South. It was her kind, who, when they came North, made it hard for the colored people already resident there. It was her kind who knew nothing of the social niceties or the polite conventions. In her own home they had been used only to coarse work and coarser manners. And they had been forbidden the chance to have intimate contact in schools and in public with white people from whom they might absorb some semblance of culture. When they did come North and get a chance to go to white schools, white theaters, and white libraries, they were too unused to them to appreciate what they were getting, and could be expected to continue their old way of life in an environment where such a way was decidedly out of place.

Emma Lou was determined to become associated only with those people who really mattered, northerners like herself or superior southerners, if there were any, who were different from whites only in so far as skin color was concerned. This girl to whom she was now about to introduce herself, was the type she had in mind, genteel, well and tastily dressed, and not ugly.

"Good morning."

Alma Martin looked up from the book she was reading, gulped in surprise, then answered, "Good morning."

Emma Lou sat down on the bench. She was congeniality itself. "Are you a new student?" she inquired of the astonished Alma, who wasn't used to this sort of thing.

"No, I'm a 'soph,'" then realizing she was expected to say more, "you're new, aren't you?"

"Oh yes" replied Emma Lou, her voice buoyant and glad. "This will be my first year."

"Do you think you will like it?"

"I'm just crazy about it already. You know," she advanced confidentially, "I've never gone to school with any colored people before."

"No?"

"No, and I am just dying to get acquainted with the colored students. Oh, my name's Emma Lou Morgan."

"And mine is Alma Martin."

They both laughed. There was a moment of silence. Alma looked at her wristwatch, then got up from the bench.

"I'm glad to have met you. I've got to see my advisor at ten-thirty. Good-bye." And she moved away gracefully.

Emma Lou was having difficulty in keeping from clapping her hands. At last she had made some headway. She had met a second-year student, one who, from all appearances, was in the know, and who, as they met from time to time, would see that she met others. In a short time Emma Lou felt that she would be in the whirl of things collegiate. She must write to her Uncle Joe immediately and let him know how well things were going. He had been right. This was the place for her to be. There had been no one in Boise worth considering. Here she was coming into contact with really superior people, intelligent, genteel, college-bred, all trying to advance themselves and their race, unconscious of intra-racial schisms caused by difference in skin color.

She mustn't stop upon meeting one person. She must find others, so once more she began her quest and almost immediately met Verne and Helen strolling down one of the campus paths. She remembered Verne as the girl who had smiled at her. She observed her more closely, and admired her pleasant dark brown face, made doubly attractive by two evenly placed dimples and a pair of large, heavily lidded, pitch black eyes. Emma Lou thought her to be much more attractive than the anemic-looking yellow girl with whom she was strolling. There was something about this second girl which made Emma Lou feel that she was not easy to approach.

"Good morning." Emma Lou had evolved a formula.

"Good morning," the two girls spoke in unison. Helen was about to walk on but Verne stopped.

"New student?" she asked.

"Yes, I am."

"So am I. I'm Verne Davis."

"I'm Emma Lou Morgan."

"And this is Helen Wheaton."

"Pleased to meet you, Miss Morgan."

"And I'm pleased to meet you, too, both of you," gushed Emma Lou. "You see, I'm from Boise, Idaho, and all through high school I was the only colored student."

"Is that so?" Helen inquired listlessly. Then turning to Verne said, "Better come on Verne if you are going to drive us out to the 'Branch.'"

"All right. We've got to run along now. We'll see you again, Miss Morgan. Good-bye."

"Good-bye," said Emma Lou and stood watching them as they went on their way. Yes, college life was going to be the thing to bring her out, the turning point in her life. She would show the people back in Boise that she did not have to be a "no-gooder" as they claimed her father had been, just because she was black. She would show all of them that a dark-skin girl could go as far in life as a fair-skin one, and that she could have as much opportunity and as much happiness. What did the color of one's skin have to do with one's mentality or native ability? Nothing whatsoever. If a black boy could get along in the world, so could a black girl, and it would take her, Emma Lou Morgan, to prove it.

With that she set out to make still more acquaintances.

Two weeks of school had left Emma Lou's mind in a chaotic state. She was unable to draw any coherent conclusions from the jumble of new things she had experienced. In addition to her own social striving, there had been the academic routine to which she had to adapt herself. She had found it all bewildering and overpowering. The university was a huge business proposition and every one in it had jobs to perform. Its bigness awed her. Its blatant reality shocked her. There was nothing romantic about going to college. It was, indeed, a serious business. One went there with a purpose and had several other purposes inculcated into one after school began. This getting an education was stern and serious, regulated and systematized, dull and unemotional.

Besides being disappointed at the drabness and lack of romance in college routine, Emma Lou was also depressed by her inability to make much headway in the matter of becoming intimately associated with her colored campus mates. They were all polite enough. They all acknowledged their introductions to her and would speak whenever they passed her, but seldom did any of them stop for a chat, and when she joined the various groups which gathered on the campus lawn between classes, she always felt excluded and out of things because she found herself unable to participate in the general conversation. They talked of things about which she knew nothing, of parties and dances, and of people she did not know. They seemed to live a life off the campus to which she was not privy, and into which they did not seem particularly anxious to introduce her.

She wondered why she never knew of the parties they talked about, and why she never received invitations to any of their affairs. Perhaps it was because she was still new and comparatively unknown to them. She felt that she must not forget that most of them had known one another for a long period of time and that it was necessary for people who "belonged" to be wary of strangers. That was it. She was still a stranger, had only been among them for about two weeks. What did she expect? Why was she so impatient?

The thought of the color question presented itself to her time and time again, but she would always dismiss it from her mind. Verne Davis was dark and she was not excluded from the sacred inner circle. In fact, she was one of the most popular colored girls on the campus. The only thing that perplexed Emma Lou was that although Verne, too, was new to the group, had just recently moved into the city, and was also just beginning her first year at the university, she had not been kept at a distance or excluded from any of the major extra-collegiate activities. Emma Lou could not understand why there should be this difference in their social acceptance. She was certainly as good as Verne.

In time Emma Lou became certain that it was because of her intimacy with Hazel that the people in the campus she really wished to be friendly with paid her so little attention. Hazel was

a veritable clown. She went scooting about the campus, cutting
capers, playing the darky for the amused white students. Any
time Hazel asked or answered a question in any of the lecture
halls, there was certain to be laughter. She had a way of phrasing
what she wished to say in a manner which was invariably laugh
provoking. The very tone and quality of her voice designated her
as a minstrel type. In the gymnasium she would do buck and
wing dances and play low-down blues on the piano. She was a
pariah among her own people because she did not seem to
know, as they knew, that Negroes could not afford to be funny
in front of white people even if that was their natural inclination.
Negroes must always be sober and serious in order to impress
white people with their adaptability and non-difference in all
salient characteristics save skin color. All of the Negro students
on the campus, except Emma Lou, laughed at her openly and
called her Topsy. Emma Lou felt sorry for her although she, too,
regretted her comic propensities and wished that she would be
less the vaudevillian and more the college student.

Besides Hazel, there was only one other person on the campus who was friendly with Emma Lou. This was Grace Giles,
also a black girl, who was registered in the School of Music. The
building in which she had her classes was located some distance
away, and Grace did not get over to the main campus grounds
very often, but when she did, she always looked for Emma Lou
and made welcome overtures of friendship. It was her second
year in the university, and yet, she, too, seemed to be on the
outside of things. She didn't seem to be invited to the parties
and dances, nor was she a member of the Greek letter sorority
which the colored girls had organized. Emma Lou asked her
why.

"Have the pledged you?" was Grace Giles' answer.

"Why no."

"And they won't either."

"Why?" Emma Lou asked surprised.

"Because you are not a high brown or half-white."

Emma Lou had thought this, too, but she had been loath to
believe it.

"You're silly, Grace. Why—Verne belongs."

"Yeah," Grace had sneered, "Verne, a bishop's daughter with plenty of coin and a big Buick. Why shouldn't they ask her?"

Emma Lou did not know what to make of this. She did not want to believe that the same color prejudice which existed among the blue veins in Boise also existed among the colored college students. Grace Giles was just hypersensitive. She wasn't taking into consideration the fact that she was not on the campus regularly and thus could not expect to be treated as if she were. Emma Lou fully believed that had Grace been a regularly enrolled student like herself, she would have found things different, and she was also certain that both she and Grace would be asked to join the sorority in due time.

But they weren't. Nor did an entire term in the school change things one whit. The Christmas holidays had come and gone and Emma Lou had not been invited to one of the many parties. She and Grace and Hazel bound themselves together and sought their extra-collegiate pleasure among people not on the campus. Hazel began to associate with a group of housemaids and mature youths who worked only when they had to, and played the pool rooms and the housemaids as long as they proved profitable. Hazel was a welcome addition to this particular group what with her car and her full pocketbook. She had never been proficient in her studies, had always found it impossible to keep pace with the other students, and, finally realizing that she did not belong and perhaps never would, had decided to "go to the devil," and be done with it.

It was not long before Hazel was absent from the campus more often than she was present. Going to cabarets and parties, and taking long drunken midnight drives made her more and more unwilling and unable to undertake the scholastic grind on the next morning. Just before the mid-term examinations, she was advised by the faculty to drop out of school until the next year, and to put herself in the hands of a tutor during the intervening period. It was evident that her background was not all that it should be; her preparatory work had not been sufficiently complete to enable her to continue in college. As it was, they told her, she was wasting her time. So Hazel disappeared from the campus and was said to have gone back to Texas. "Serves her right, glad she's gone," was the verdict of her colored campus fellows.

The Christmas holidays for Emma Lou were dull and uneventful. The people she lived with were rheumatic and not much given to Yuletide festivities. It didn't seem like Christmas to Emma Lou anyway. There was no snow on the ground, and the sun was shining as brightly and as warmly as it had shone during the late summer and early autumn months. The wild geraniums still flourished, the orange trees were blossoming, and the whole southland seemed to be preparing for the annual New Year's Day Tournament of Roses parade in Pasadena.

Emma Lou received a few presents from home, and a Christmas greeting card from Grace Giles. That was all. On Christmas Day she and Grace attended church in the morning, and spent the afternoon at the home of one of Grace's friends. Emma Lou never liked the people to whom Grace introduced her. They were a dull, commonplace lot for the most part, people from Georgia, Grace's former home, untutored people who didn't really matter. Emma Lou borrowed a word from her grandmother and classified them as "fuddlers," because they seemed to fuddle everything—their language, their clothes, their attempts at politeness, and their efforts to appear more intelligent than they really were.

The holidays over, Emma Lou returned to school a little reluctantly. She wasn't particularly interested in her studies, but having nothing else to do kept up in them and made high grades. Meanwhile she had been introduced to a number of young men and gone out with them occasionally. They, too, were friends of Grace's and of the came caliber as Grace's other friends. There were no college boys among them except Joe Lane who was flunking out of the School of Dentistry. He did not interest Emma Lou. As it was with Joe, so it was with all the other boys. She invariably picked them to pieces when they took her out, and remained so impassive to their emotional advances that they were soon glad to be on their way and let her be. Emma Lou was determined not to go out of her class, determined either to associate with the "right sort of people" or else to remain to herself.

Had any one asked Emma Lou what she meant by the "right sort of people" she would have found herself at a loss for a comprehensive answer. She really didn't know. She had a vague idea that those people on the campus who practically ignored her were the only people with whom she should associate. These people, for the most part, were children of fairly well-to-do families from Louisiana, Texas, and Georgia, who, having made nest eggs, had journeyed to the West for the same reasons that her grandparents at an earlier date had also journeyed West. They wanted to live where they would have greater freedom and greater opportunity for both their children and themselves. Then, too, the World War had given impetus to this westward movement. There was more industry in the West and thus more chances for money to be made, and more opportunities to invest this money profitably in property and progeny.

The greater number of them were either mulattoes or light brown in color. In their southern homes they had segregated themselves from their darker skinned brethren and they continued this practice in the North. They went to Episcopal, Presbyterian, or Catholic churches, and though they were not as frankly organized into a blue vein society as were the Negroes of Boise, they nevertheless kept more or less to themselves. They were not insistent that their children get "whiter and whiter, every generation," but they did want to keep their children and grandchildren from having dark complexions. A light brown was the favored color; it was therefore found expedient to exercise caution when it came to mating.

The people who, in Emma Lou's phrase, really mattered, the business men, the doctors, the lawyers, the dentists, the more moneyed Pullman porters, hotel waiters, bank janitors and majordomos, in fact all of the Negro leaders and members of the Negro upper class, were either light skinned themselves or else had light-skinned wives. A wife of dark complexion was considered a handicap unless she was particularly charming, wealthy, or beautiful. An ordinary-looking dark woman was no suitable mate for a Negro man of prominence. The college youths on whom the future of the race depended practiced this precept of their elders religiously. It was not the girls in the school who were prejudiced—they had no reason to be, but they knew full well that the boys with whom they wished to associate, their future husbands, would not tolerate a dark girl unless she had, like Verne, many things to compensate for her dark skin. Thus they did not encourage a friendship with some one whom they knew didn't belong. Thus they did not even pledge girls like Grace, Emma Lou, and Hazel into their sorority, for they knew that it would make them the more miserable to attain the threshold only to have the door shut in their faces.

Summer vacation time came and Emma Lou went back to Boise. She was thoroughly discouraged and depressed. She had been led to expect so much pleasure from her first year in college and in Los Angeles; but she had found that the people in large cities were after all no different from people in small cities. Her Uncle Joe had been wrong—her mother and grandmother had been right. There was no place in the world for a dark girl.

Being at home depressed her all the more. There was absolutely nothing for her to do nor any place for her to go. For a month or more she just lingered around the house, bored by her mother's constant and difficult attempts to be maternal, and irritated by her Cousin Buddie's freshness. Adolescent boys were such a nuisance. The only bright spot on the horizon was the Sunday School Union picnic scheduled to be held during the latter part of July. It was always the crowning social event of the summer season among the colored citizens of Boise. Both the Methodist and Baptist missions cooperated in this affair and had their numbers augmented by all the denominationally unattached members of the community. It was always a gala, democratic affair designed to provide a pleasant day in the out-of-doors. It was, besides the annual dance fostered by the local chapters of the Masons and the Elks, the only big community gathering to which the entire colored population of Boise looked forward.

Picnic day came, and Emma Lou accompanied her mother, her uncle, and her cousin to Bedney's Meadow, a green, heavily forested acre of park land, which lay on the outskirts of the city, surrounded on three sides by verdant foothills. The day went by pleasantly enough. There were the usually heavily laden wooden tables, to which all adjourned in the late afternoon, and there were foot races, games, and canoeing.

Emma Lou took part in all these activities and was surprised to find that she was having a good time. The company was congenial, and she found that since she had gone away to college she had become somewhat of a personage. Every one seemed to be going out of his way to be congenial to her. The blue veins did not rule this affair. They were, in fact, only a minority element, and, for one of the few times of the year, mingled freely and unostentatiously with their lower-caste brethren.

All during the day, Emma Lou found herself paired off with a chap by the name of Weldon Taylor. In the evening they went for a stroll up the precipitous footpaths in the hills which grew up from the meadow. Weldon Taylor was a newcomer in the West trying to earn sufficient money to re-enter an eastern school and finish his medical education. Emma Lou rather liked him. She admired his tall, slender body, the deep burnish of his bronze-colored skin, and his mass of black curly hair. Here, thought Emma, is the type of man I like. Only she did wish that his skin had been colored light brown instead of dark brown. It was better if she was to marry that she did not get a dark skin mate. Her children must not suffer as she had and would suffer.

The two talked of commonplace things as they walked along, comparing notes of their school experiences, and talking of their professors and their courses of study. It was dusk and the sun had disappeared behind the snow capped mountains. The sky was a colorful haze, a master artist's canvas on which the colors of day were slowly being dominated by the colors of night. Weldon drew Emma Lou off the little path they had been following, and led her to a huge boulder which jutted out, elbow like, from the side of a hill, and which was hidden from the meadow below by clumps of bushes. They sat down, his arm slipped around her waist, and, as the darkness of night more and more conquered the evanescent light of day, their lips met, and Emma Lou grew lax in Weldon's arms. . . .

When they finally returned to the picnic grounds all had left save a few stragglers like themselves who had sauntered away from the main party. These made up a laughing, half-embarrassed group, who collected their baskets and reluctantly withdrew from the meadow to begin the long walk back to their homes. Emma Lou and Weldon soon managed to fall at the end of the procession, walking along slowly, his arm around her waist. Emma Lou felt an ecstasy surging through her at this moment greater than she had ever known before. This had been her first intimate sexual contact, her first awareness of the physical and emotional pleasures able to be enjoyed by two human beings, a woman and a man. She felt some magnetic force drawing her to this man walking by her side, which made her long to feel the pleasure of his body against hers, made her want to know once more the pleasure which had attended the union of their lips, the touching of their tongues. It was with a great effort that she walked along apparently calm, for inside she was seething. Her body had become a kennel for clashing, screaming compelling urges and desires. She loved this man. She had submitted herself to him, had gladly suffered momentary physical pain in order to be introduced into a new and incomparably satisfying paradise.

Not for one moment did Emma Lou consider regretting the loss of her virtue, not once did any of her mother's and grandmother's warnings and solicitations revive themselves and cause her conscience to plague her. She had finally found herself a mate; she had finally come to know the man she should love, some inescapable force had drawn them together, had made them feel from the first moment of their introduction that they belonged to one another, and that they were destined to explore nature's mysteries together. Life was not so cruel after all. There were some compensatory moments. Emma Lou believed that at last she had found happiness, that at last she had found her man.

Of course, she wasn't going to go back to school. She was going to stay in Boise, marry Weldon, and work with him until they should have sufficient money to go East, where he could re-enter medical school, and she could keep a home for him and spur him on. A glorious panorama of the future unrolled itself in her mind. There were no black spots in it, no shadows, nothing but luminous landscapes, ethereal in substance.

It was the way of Emma Lou always to create her worlds within her own mind without taking under consideration the fact that other people and other elements, not contained within herself, would also have to aid in their molding. She had lived to herself for so long, had been shut out from the stream of things in which she was interested for such a long period during the formative years of her life, that she considered her own imaginative powers omniscient. Thus she constructed a future world of love on one isolated experience, never thinking for the moment that the other party concerned might not be of the same mind. She had been lifted into a superlatively perfect emotional and physical state. It was unthinkable, incongruous, that Weldon, too, had not been similarly lifted. He had for the moment shared her ecstasy; therefore, according to Emma Lou's line of reasoning, he would as effectively share what she imagined would be the fruits of that ecstatic moment.

The next two weeks passed quickly and happily. Weldon called on her almost every night, took her for long walks, and thrilled her with his presence and his love making. Never before in her life had Emma Lou been so happy. She forgot all the sad past. Forgot what she had hitherto considered the tragedy of her birth, forgot the social isolation of her childhood and of her college days. What did being black, what did the antagonistic mental attitudes of the people who really mattered mean when she was in love? Her mother and her Uncle Joe were so amazed at the change in her that they became afraid, sensed danger, and began to be on the lookout for some untoward development; for hitherto Emma Lou had always been sullen and morose and impertinent to all around the house. She had always been the anti-social creature they had caused her to feel she was, and since she was made to feel that she was a misfit, she had encroached upon their family life and sociabilities only to the extent that being in the house made necessary. But now she was changed—she had become a vibrant, joyful being. There was always a smile on her face, always a note of joy in her voice as she spoke or sang. She even made herself agreeable to her

Cousin Buddie, who in the past she had either ignored or else barely tolerated.

"She must be in love, Joe," her mother half whined.

"That's good," he answered laconically. "It probably won't last long. It will serve to take her mind off herself."

"But suppose she gets foolish?" Jane had insisted, remembering no doubt her own foolishness, during a like period of her own life, with Emma Lou's father.

"She'll take care of herself," Joe had returned with an assurance he did not feel. He, too, was worried, but he was also pleased at the change in Emma Lou. His only fear was that perhaps in the end she would make herself more miserable than she had ever been before. He did not know much about this Weldon fellow, who seemed to be a reliable enough chap, but no one had any way of discerning whether or not his intentions were entirely honorable. It was best, thought Joe, not to worry about such things. If, for the present, Emma Lou was more happy than she had ever been before, there would be time enough to worry about the future when its problems materialized.

"Don't you worry about Emma Lou. She's got sense."

"But, Joe, suppose she does forget herself with this man? He is studying to be a doctor and he may not want a wife, especially when. . . ."

"Damnit, Jane!" her brother snapped at her. "Do you think every one is like you? The boy seems to like her."

"Men like any one they can use, but you know as well as I that no professional man is going to marry a woman as dark as Emma Lou."

"Men marry any one they love, just as you and I did."

"But I was foolish."

"Well?"

"That's right—Be unconcerned. That's right—Let her go to the devil. There's no hope for her anyway. Oh—why—why did I marry Jim Morgan?" and she had gone into the usual crying fit which inevitably followed this self-put question.

Then, without any warning, as if to put an end to all problems, Weldon decided to become a Pullman porter. He explained to Emma Lou that he could make more money on the railroad

than he could as a hotel waiter in Boise. It was necessary for his
future that he make as much money as possible in as short a
time as possible. Emma Lou saw the logic of this and agreed
that it was the best possible scheme, until she realized that it
meant his going away from Boise, perhaps forever. Oakland,
California, was to be his headquarters, and he, being a new man,
would not have a regular run, It was possible that he might be
sent to different sections of the country each and every time he
made a trip. There was no way of his knowing before he reported for duty just where he might be sent. It might be Boise or
Palm Beach or Albany or New Orleans. One never knew. That
was the life of the road, and one had to accept it in order to
make money.

It made Emma Lou shiver to hear him talk so dispassionately
about the matter. There didn't seem to be the least note of
regret in his voice, the least suggestion that he hated to leave her
or that he would miss her, and, for the first time since the night
of their physical union, Emma Lou began to realize that perhaps
after all he did not feel toward her as she did toward him. He
couldn't possibly love her as much as she loved him, and, at the
same time, remain so unconcerned about having to part from
her. There was something radically wrong here, something con-
clusive and unexpected which was going to hurt her, going to
plunge her back into unhappiness once more. Then she realized
that not once had he ever spoken of marriage or even hinted
that their relationship would continue indefinitely. He had said
that he loved her, he had treated her kindly, and had seemed as
thrilled as she over their physical contacts. But now it seemed
that since he was no longer going to be near her, no longer going
to need her body, he had forgotten that he loved her. It was then
that all the old preachments of her mother and grandmother
were resurrected and began to swirl through her mind. Hadn't
she been warned that men don't marry black girls? Hadn't she
been told that they would only use her for their sexual conve-
nience? That was the case with Weldon! He had taken up with
her only because he was a stranger in the town and lonesome for
a companion, and she, like a damn fool had submitted herself to
him! And now that he was about to better his condition, about

to go some place where he would have a wider circle of acquaintances, she was to be discarded and forgotten.

Thus Emma Lou reasoned to herself and grew bitter. It never occurred to her that the matter of her color had never once entered the mind of Weldon. Not once did she consider that he was acting toward her as he would have acted toward any girl under similar circumstances, whether her face had been white, yellow, brown, or black. Emma Lou did not understand that Weldon was just a selfish normal man and not a color-prejudiced one, at least not while he was resident in a community where the girls were few, and there were none of his college friends about to tease him for liking "dark meat." She did not know that for over a year he had been traveling about from town to town, always seeking a place where money was more plentiful and more easily saved, and that in every town he had managed to find a girl, or girls, who made it possible for him to continue his grind without being totally deprived of pleasurable moments. To Emma Lou there could only be one reason for his not having loved her as she had loved him. She was a black girl and no professional man could afford to present such a wife in the best society. It was the tragic feature of her life once more asserting itself. There could be no happiness in life for any woman whose face was as black as hers.

Believing this more intensely than ever before Emma Lou yet felt that she must manage in some way to escape both home and school. That she must find happiness somewhere else. The idea her Uncle Joe had given her about the provinciality of people in small towns re-entered her mind. After all Los Angeles, too, was a small-town mentally, peopled by mentally small southern Negroes. It was no better than Boise. She was now determined to go East where life was more cosmopolitan and people were more civilized. To this end she begged her mother and uncle to send her East to school.

"Can't you ever be satisfied?"

"Now Jane," Joe as usual was trying to keep the peace—

"Now Jane, nothing! I never saw such an ungrateful child."

"I'm not ungrateful. I'm just unhappy. I don't like that school. I don't want to go there any more."

"Well, you'll either go there or else stay home." Thus Jane ended the discussion and could not be persuaded to re-open it.

And rather than remain home Emma Lou returned to Los Angeles and spent another long, miserable, uneventful year in the University of Southern California, drawing more and more within herself and becoming more and more bitter. When vacation time came again she got herself a job as a maid in a theater, rather than return home, and studied stenography during her spare hours. School began again and Emma Lou re-entered with more determination than ever to escape should the chance present itself. It did, and once more Emma Lou fled into an unknown town to escape the haunting chimera of intra-racial color prejudice.

Part 2

Harlem

Emma Lou turned her face away from the wall, and quizzically squinted her dark, pea-like eyes at the recently closed door. Then, sitting upright, she strained her ears, trying to hear the familiar squeak of the impudent floor boards, as John tiptoed down the narrow hallway toward the outside door. Finally, after she had heard the closing click of the double-barreled police lock, she climbed out of the bed, picked up a brush from the bureau, and attempted to smooth the sensuous disorder of her hair. She had just recently had it bobbed, boyishly bobbed, because she thought this style narrowed and enhanced the fulsome lines of her facial features. She was always trying to emphasize those things about her that seemed, somehow, to atone for her despised darkness, and she never faced the mirror without speculating upon how good-looking she might have been had she not been so black.

Mechanically, she continued the brushing of her hair, stopping every once in a while to give it an affectionate caress. She was intensely in love with her hair, in love with its electric vibrancy and its unruly buoyance. Yet, this morning, she was irritated because it seemed so determined to remain disordered, so determined to remain a stubborn and unnecessary reminder of the night before. Why, she wondered, should one's physical properties always insist upon appearing awry after a night of stolen or forbidden pleasure? But not being anxious to find an answer, she dismissed the question from her mind, put on a stocking-cap, and jumped back into the bed.

She began to think about John, poor John who felt so hurt
because she had told him that he could not spend any more days
or nights with her. She wondered if she should pity him, for she
was certain that he would miss the nights more than he would
the days. Yet, she must not be too harsh in her conclusions, for,
after all, there had only been two nights, which, she smiled to
herself, was a pretty good record for a newcomer to Harlem.
She had been in New York now for five weeks, and it seemed
like, well, just a few days. Five weeks—thirty-five days and
thirty-five nights, and of these nights John had had two. And
now he sulked because she would not promise him another;
because she had, in fact, boldly told him that there could be no
more between them. Mischievously, she wished now that she
could have seen the expression on his face, when, after seeming
moments of mutual ecstasy, she had made this cold, manifesto-
like announcement. But the room had been dark, and so was
John. Ugh!

She had only written home twice. This, of course, seemed
quite all right to her. She was not concerned about any one
there except her Uncle Joe, and she reasoned that since he was
preparing to marry again, he would be far too busy to think
much about her. All that worried her was the pitiful spectacle of
her mother, her uncle, and her cousin trying to make up lies to
tell inquiring friends. Well, she would write today, that is, if she
did not start to work, and she must get up at eight o'clock—was
the alarm set?—and hie herself to an employment agency. She
had only thirty-five dollars left in the bank, and, unless it was
replenished, she might have to rescind her avowals to John in
order to get her room rent paid.

She must go to sleep for another hour, for she wished to look
"pert" when she applied for a job, especially the kind of job she
wanted, and she must get the kind of job she wanted in order to
show those people in Boise and Los Angeles that she had been
perfectly justified in leaving school, home, and all, to come to
New York. They all wondered why she had come. So did she,
now that she was here. But at the moment of leaving she would
have gone any place to escape having to remain in that hateful
Southern California college, or having to face the more dreaded

alternative of returning home. Home? It had never been a home.

It did seem strange, this being Harlem when only a few weeks before she had been over three thousand miles away. Time and distance—strange things, immutable, yet conquerable. But was time conquerable? Hadn't she read or heard somewhere that all things were subject to time, even God? Yet, once she was there and now she was here. But even at that she hadn't conquered time. What was that line in Cullen's verse, "I run, but Time's abreast with me"? She had only traversed space and defied distance. This suggested a more banal, if a less arduous thought tangent. She had defied more than distance, she had defied parental restraint—still there hadn't been much of that— friendly concern—there had been still less of that, and malicious, meddlesome gossip, of which there had been plenty. And she still found herself unable to understand why two sets of people in two entirely different communities should seemingly become almost hysterically excited because she, a woman of twenty-one, with three years' college training and ample sophistication in the ways of sex and self-support, had decided to take a job as an actress' maid in order to get to New York. They had never seemed interested in her before.

Now she wondered why had she been so painfully anxious to come to New York. She had given as a consoling reason to inquisitive friends and relatives, school. But she knew too well that she had no intentions of ever re-entering school. She had had enough of that school in Los Angeles, and her experiences there, more than anything else, had caused this foolhardy hegira to Harlem. She had been desperately driven to escape, and had she not escaped in this manner she might have done something else much more mad.

Emma Lou closed her eyes once more, and tried to sublimate her mental reverie into a sleep-inducing lullaby. Most of all, she wanted to sleep. One had to look "pert" when one sought a job, and she wondered if eight o'clock would find her looking any more "pert" than she did at this present moment. What had caused her to urge John to spend what she knew would be his last night with her when she was determined to be at her best

the following morning! O, what the hell was the use? She was
going to sleep.

The alarm had not yet rung, but Emma Lou was awakened
gradually by the sizzling and smell of fried and warmed-over
breakfast, by the raucous early morning wranglings and window
to window greetings, and by the almost constant squeak of those
impudent hall floor boards as the various people in her apartment raced one another to the kitchen or to the bathroom or to
the front door. How could Harlem be so happily busy, so alive
and merry at eight o'clock. Eight o'clock? The alarm rang.
Emma Lou scuttled out of the bed and put on her clothes.

An hour later, looking as "pert" as possible, she entered the
first employment agency she came to on 135th Street, between
Lenox and Seventh Avenues. It was her first visit to such an
establishment and she was particularly eager to experience this
phase of a working girl's life. Her first four weeks in Harlem had
convinced her that jobs were easy to find, for she had noticed
that there were three or four employment agencies to every
block in business Harlem. Assuring herself in this way that she
would experience little difficulty in obtaining a permanent and
tasty position, Emma Lou had abruptly informed Mazelle
Lindsay that she was leaving her employ.

"But, child," her employer had objected, "I feel responsible
for you. Your—your mother! Don't be preposterous. How can
you remain in New York alone?"

Emma Lou had smiled, asked for her money once more,
closed her ears to all protest, bid the chagrined woman good-
bye, and joyously loafed for a week.

Now, with only thirty-five dollars left in the bank, she thought
that she had best find a job—find a job and then finish seeing
New York. Of course she had seen much already. She had seen
John—and he—oh, damn John, she wanted a job.

"What can I do for you?" the harassed woman at the desk was
trying to be polite.

"I—I want a job." R-r-ring. The telephone insistently peti-
tioned for attention, giving Emma Lou a moment of respite,
while the machine-like woman wearily shouted monosyllabic

answers into the instrument, and, at the same time, tried to hush the many loud-mouthed men and women in the room, all, it seemed, trying to out-talk one another. While waiting, Emma Lou surveyed her fellow job-seekers. Seedy lot, was her verdict. Perhaps I should have gone to a more high-toned place. Well, this will do for the moment.

"What kinda job d'ye want?"

"I prefer," Emma Lou had rehearsed these lines for a week, "a stenographic position in some colored business or professional office."

"'Ny experience?"

"No, but I took two courses in business college, during school vacations. I have a certificate of competency."

"'Ny reference?"

"No New York ones."

"Where'd ya work before?"

"I—I just came to the city."

"Where'd ya come . . . ?" R-r-ring. That telephone mercifully reiterated its insistent blare, and, for a moment, kept that pesky woman from droning out more insulting queries.

"Now," she had finished again, "where'd ya come from?"

"Los Angeles."

"Ummm. What other kind of work would ya take?"

"Anything congenial."

"Waal, what is that, dishwashing, day work, nurse girl?"

Didn't this damn woman know what congenial meant? And why should a Jewish woman be in charge of a Negro employment agency in Harlem?

"Waal, girlie, others waiting."

"I'll consider anything you may have on hand, if stenographic work is not available."

"Wanta work part-time?"

"I'd rather not."

"Awright. Sit down. I'll call you in a moment."

"What can I do for you, young man?" Emma Lou was dismissed.

She looked for a place to sit down, and, finding none, walked across the narrow room to the window, hoping to get a breath of fresh air, and at the same time an advantageous position from which to watch the drama of some one else playing the role of a job-seeker.

"R-r-ring."

"Whadda want? Wait a minute. Oh, Sadie."

A heavy-set, dark-brown-skinned woman, with full, flopping breasts, and extra-wide buttocks, squirmed off a too narrow chair, and bashfully wobbled up to the desk.

"Wanta' go to a place on West End Avenue? Part-time cleaning, fifty cents an hour, nine rooms, yeah? All right? Hello, gotta girl on the way. 'Bye. Two and a half, Sadie. Here's the address. Run along now, don't idle."

R-r-ring. "'Lo, yes. What? Come down to the office. I can't sell jobs over the wire."

Emma Lou began to see the humor in this sordid situation, began to see something extremely comic in all these plaintive, pitiful-appearing colored folk, some greasy, some neat, some fat, some slim, some brown, some black (why was there only one mulatto in this crowd?), boys and men, girls and women, all single-filing up to the desk, laconically answering laconic questions, impertinently put, showing thanks or sorrow or indifference, as their cases warranted, paying off promptly, or else seeking credit, the while the Jewish overseer of the dirty, dingy office asserted and re-asserted her superiority.

Some one on the outside pushed hard on the warped door. Protestingly it came open, and the small stuffy room was filled with the odor and presence of a stout, black lady dressed in a greasy gingham housedress, still damp in the front from splashing dishwater. On her head was a tight turban, too round for the rather long outlines of her head. Beneath this turban could be seen short and wiry stands of recently straightened hair. And her face! Emma Lou sought to observe it more closely, sought to fathom how so much grease could gather on one woman's face. But her head reeled. The room was vile with noise and heat and body-smells, and this woman—

"Hy, Rosie, yer late. Got a job for ya."

The greasy-faced black woman grinned broadly, licked her pork chop lips, and, with a flourish, sat down in an empty chair beside the desk. Emma Lou stumbled over three pairs of number ten shoes, pulled open the door, and fled into the street.

She walked hurriedly for about twenty-five yards, then slowed down and tried to collect her wits. Telephone bells echoed in her ears. Sour smells infested her nostrils. She looked up and discovered that she had paused in front of two garbage cans, waiting on the curbstone for the scavenger's truck.

Irritated, she turned around and re-traced her steps. There were few people on the street. The early morning work crowds had already been swallowed by the subway kiosks on Lenox Avenue, and it was too early for the afternoon idlers. Yet there was much activity, much passing to and fro. One Hundred and Thirty-Fifth Street, Emma Lou mumbled to herself as she strolled along. How she had longed to see it, and what a different thoroughfare she had imagined it to be! Her eyes sought the opposite side of the street and blinked at a line of monotonously regular fire escape-decorated tenement buildings. She thanked whoever might be responsible for the architectural difference of the Y.M.C.A., for the streaming bit of Seventh Avenue near by, and for the arresting corner of the newly constructed teachers' college building, which dominated the hill three blocks away, and cast its shadows on the verdure of the terraced park beneath.

But she was looking for a job. Sour smells assailed her nostrils once more. Rasping voices. Pleading voices. Tired voices. Domineering voices. And the insistent ring of the telephone bell all re-echoed in her head and beat against her eardrums. She must have staggered, for a passing youth eyed her curiously, and shouted to no one in particular, "oh, *no*, now." Some one else laughed. They thought she was drunk. Tears blurred her eyes. She wanted to run, but resolutely she kept her steady, slow pace, lifted her head a little higher, and, seeing another employment agency, faltered for a moment, then went in.

This agency, like the first, occupied the ground-floor front of a tenement house, three-quarters of the way between Lenox and Seventh Avenue. It was cagey and crowded, and there was a great conversational hubbub as Emma Lou entered. In the rear of the room was a door marked "private," to the left of this door was a desk, littered with papers and index cards, before which was a swivel chair. The rest of the room was lined with a miscellaneous assortment of chairs, three rows of them, tied together and trying to be precise despite their varying sizes and shapes. A single window looked out upon the street and the Y.M.C.A. building opposite.

All of the chairs were occupied and three people stood lined up by the desk. Emma Lou fell in at the end of this line. There was nothing else to do. In fact, it was all she could do after entering. Not another person could have been squeezed into that room from the outside. This office, too, was noisy and hot and pregnant with clashing body smells. The buzzing electric fan, in a corner over the desk, with all its whirring, could not stir up a breeze.

The rear door opened. A slender, light-brown-skinned boy, his high cheekbones decorated with blackheads, his slender form accentuated by a tight-fitting jazz suit of the high-waistline, one-button coat, bell-bottom trouser variety, emerged smiling broadly, cap in one hand, a slip of pink paper in the other. He elbowed his way to the outside door and was gone.

"Musta got a job," somebody commented. "It's about time," came from some one else, "he said, he'd been sittin' here a week."

The rear door opened again and a lady with a youthful brown face and iron-gray hair sauntered in and sat down in the swivel chair before the desk. Immediately all talk in the outer office ceased. An air of anticipation seemed to pervade the room. All eyes were turned toward her.

For a moment she fingered a pack of red index cards, then, as if remembering something, turned around in her chair and called out:

"Mrs. Blake says for all elevator men to stick around."

There was a shuffling of feet and a settling back into chairs. Noticing this, Emma Lou counted six elevator men and wondered if she was right. Again the brown aristocrat with the tired voice spoke up:

"Day workers come back at one-thirty. Won't be nothing doin' 'til then."

Four women, all carrying newspaper packages, got out of their chairs, and edged their way toward the door, murmuring to one another as they went, "I ain't fixin' to come back."

"Ah, she keeps you hyar."

They were gone.

Two of the people standing in line sat down, the third approached the desk, Emma Lou close behind.

"I wantsa—"

"What kind of job do you want?"

Couldn't people ever finish what they had to say?

"Porter or dishwashing, lady."

"Are you registered with us?"

"No'm."

"Have a seat. I'll call you in a moment."

The boy looked frightened, but he found a seat and slid into it gratefully. Emma Lou approached the desk. The woman's cold eyes appraised her. She must have been pleased with what she saw for her eyes softened and her smile reappeared. Emma Lou smiled, too. Maybe she was "pert" after all. The tailored blue suit—

"What can I do for you?"

The voice with the smile wins. Emma Lou was encouraged.

"I would like stenographic work."

"Experienced?"

"Yes." It was so much easier to say than "no."

"Good."

Emma Lou held tightly to her under-arm bag.

"We have something that would just about suit you. Just a minute, and I'll let you see Mrs. Blake."

The chair squeaked and was eased of its burden. Emma Lou thought she heard a telephone ringing somewhere in the distance, or perhaps it was the clang of the street car that had just passed, heading for Seventh Avenue. The people in the room began talking again.

"Dat last job." "Boy, she was dressed right down to the bricks."

"And I told him . . ." "Yeah, we went to see 'Flesh and the Devil.'" "Some parteee." "I just been here a week."

Emma Lou's mind became jumbled with incoherent wisps of thought. Her left foot beat a nervous tattoo upon a sagging floor board. The door opened. The gray-haired lady with the smile in her voice beckoned, and Emma Lou walked into the private office of Mrs. Blake.

Four people in the room. The only window facing a brick wall on the outside. Two telephones, both busy. A good-looking young man, fingering papers in a filing cabinet, while he talked over one of the telephones. The lady from the outer office. Another lady, short and brown, like butterscotch, talking over a desk telephone and motioning for Emma Lou to sit down. Blur of high-powered electric lights, brighter than daylight. The butterscotch lady hanging up the receiver.

"I'm through with you young man." Crisp tones. Metal, warm in spite of itself.

"Well, I ain't through with you." The fourth person was speaking. Emma Lou had hardly noticed him before. Sullen face. Dull black eyes in watery sockets. The nose flat, the lips thick and pouting. One hand clutching a derby, the other clenched, bearing down on the corner of the desk.

"I have no intention of arguing with you. I've said my say. Go on outside. When a cook's job comes in, you can have it. That's all I can do."

"No, it ain't all you can do."

"Well, I'm not going to give you your fee back."

The lady from the outside office returns to her post. The good-looking young man is at the telephone again.

"Why not, I'm entitled to it?"

"No, you're not. I send you on a job, the man asks you to do something, you walk out, Mister Big I-am. Then, show up here two days later and want your fee back. No siree."

"I didn't walk out."

"The man says you did."

"Aw, sure, he'd say anything. I told him I came there to be a cook, not a waiter. I—"

"It was your place to do as he said, then, if not satisfied, to come here and tell me so."

"I am here."

"All right now. I'm tired of this. Take either of two courses—go on outside and wait until a job comes in or else go down to the license bureau and tell them your story. They'll investigate. If I'm right—"

"You know you ain't right."

"Not according to you, no, but by law, yes. That's all."

Telephone ringing. Warm metal whipping words into it. The good-looking young man yawning. He looks like a Y.M.C.A. secretary. The butterscotch woman speaking to Emma Lou:

"You're a stenographer?"

"Yes."

"I have a job in a real estate office, nice firm, nice people. Fill out this card. Here's a pen."

"Mrs. Blake, you know you ain't doin' right."

Why didn't this man either shut up or get out?

"I told you what to do. Now please do one or the other. You've taken up enough of my time. The license bureau—"

"You know I ain't goin' down there. I'd rather you keep the fee, if you think it will do you any good."

"I only keep what belongs to me. I've found out that's the best policy."

Why should they want three people for reference? Where had she worked before? Lies. Los Angeles was far away.

"Then, if a job comes in you'll give it to me?"

"That's what I've been trying to tell you."

"Awright." And finally he went out.

Mrs. Blake grinned across the desk at Emma Lou. "Your folks won't do, honey."

"Do you have many like that?"

The card was made out. Mrs. Blake had it in her hand. Telephones ringing, both at once. Loud talking in the outer office. Lies. Los Angeles was far away. I can bluff. Mrs. Blake had finished reading over the card.

"Just came to New York, eh?"

"Yes."

"Like it better than Los Angeles?"

The good-looking young man turned around and stared at her coldly. Now he did resemble a Y.M.C.A. secretary. The lady

from the outer office came in again. There was a triple criss-
cross conversation carried on. It ended. The short bob-haired
butterscotch boss gave Emma Lou instructions and information
about her prospective position. She was half heard. Sixteen dollars a week. Is that all? Work from nine to five. Address on card.
Corner of 139th Street, left side of the avenue. Dismissal.
Smiles and good luck. Pay the lady outside five dollars. Awkward,
flustered moments. Then the entrance door and 135th Street
once more. Emma Lou was on her way to get a job.

She walked briskly to the corner, crossed the street, and
turned north on Seventh Avenue. Her hopes were high, her
mind a medley of pleasing mental images. She visualized herself
trim and pert in her blue tailored suit being secretary to some
well-groomed Negro business man. There had not been many
such in the West, and she was eager to know and admire one.
There would be other girls in the office, too, girls who, like herself, were college trained and reared in cultural homes, and
through these fellow workers she would meet still other girls
and men, get in with the right sort of people.

She continued daydreaming as she went her way, being practical only at such fleeting moments when she would wonder—
would she be able to take dictation at the required rate of
speed? —would her fingers be nimble enough on the keyboard
of the typewriter? Oh, bother. It wouldn't take her over one day
to adapt herself to her new job.

A street crossing. Traffic delayed her and she was conscious
of a man, a blurred tan image, speaking to her. He was ignored.
Everything was to be ignored save the address digits on the
buildings. Everything was secondary to the business at hand.
Let traffic pass, let men aching for flirtations speak, let Seventh
Avenue be spangled with forenoon sunshine and shadow, and
polka-dotted with still or moving human forms. She was going
to have a job. The rest of the world could go to hell.

Emma Lou turned into a four-story brick building and sped
up one flight of stairs. The rooms were not numbered and
directing signs in the hallway only served to confuse. But Emma
Lou was not to be delayed. She rushed back and forth from door

to door on the first floor, then to the second, until she finally found the office she was looking for.

Angus and Brown were an old Harlem firm. They had begun business during the first decade of the century, handling property for a while in New York's far-famed San Juan Hill district. When the Negro population had begun to need more and better homes, Angus and Brown had led the way in buying real estate in what was to be Negro Harlem. They had been fighters, unscrupulous and canny. They had revealed a perverse delight in seeing white people rush pell-mell from the neighborhood in which they obtained homes for their colored clients. They had bought three six-story tenement buildings on 140th Street, and, when the white tenants had been slow in moving, had personally dispossessed them, and, in addition, had helped their incoming Negro tenants fight fistic battles in the streets and hallways, and legal battles in the court.

Now they were a substantial firm, grown fat and satisfied. Junior real estate men got their business for them. They held the whip. Their activities were many and varied. Politics and fraternal activities occupied more of their hectic days. Now they sat back and took it easy.

Emma Lou opened the door to their office, consisting of one medium-sized outer room overlooking Seventh Avenue. There were two girls in the outer office. One was busy at a typewriter; the other was gazing over her desk through a window into the aristocratic tree-lined city lane of 139th Street. Both looked up expectantly. Emma Lou noticed the powdered smoothness of their fair skins and the marcelled waviness of their shingled brown hair. Were they sisters? Hardly, for their features were in no way similar. Yet that skin color and that brown hair—.

"Can I do something for you?" The idle one spoke, and the other ceased her peck-peck-pecking on the typewriter keys. Emma Lou was buoyant.

"I'm from Mrs. Blake's employment agency."

"Oh," from both. And they exchanged glances. Emma Lou thought she saw a quickly suppressed smile from the fairer of the two as she hastily resumed her typing. Then——

"Sit down a moment, won't you, please? Mr. Angus is out,

but I'll inform Mr. Brown that you are here." She picked a powder puff from an open side drawer in her desk, patted her nose and cheeks, then got up and crossed the office to enter cubby hole number one. Emma Lou observed that she, too, looked "pert" in a trim, blue suit and high-heeled patent leather oxfords——

"Mr. Brown?" She had opened the door.

"Come in Grace. What is it?" The door was closed.

Emma Lou felt nervous. Something in the pit of her stomach seemed to flutter. Her pulse raced. Her eyes gleamed and a smile of anticipation spread over her face, despite her efforts to appear dignified and suave. The typist continued her work. From the cubby hole came a murmur of voices, one feminine and affected, the other masculine and coarse. Through the open window came direct sounds and vagrant echoes of traffic noises from Seventh Avenue. Now the two in the cubby hole were laughing, and the girl at the typewriter seemed to be smiling to herself as she worked.

What did this mean? Nothing, silly. Don't be so sensitive. Emma Lou's eyes sought the pictures on the wall. There was an early-twentieth-century photographic bust-portrait, encased in a beveled glass frame, of a heavy-set good-looking, brown-skinned man. She admired his mustache. Men didn't seem to take pride in such hirsute embellishments now. Mustaches these days were abbreviated and limp. They no longer were virile enough to dominate and make a man's face appear more strong. Rather, they were only significant patches weakly keeping the nostrils from merging with the upper lip.

Emma Lou wondered if that was Mr. Brown. He had a brown face and wore a brown suit. No, maybe that was Mr. Angus, and perhaps that was Mr. Brown on the other side of the room, in the square, enlarged Kodak print, a slender yellow man, standing beside a motor car, looking as if he wished to say, "Yeah, this is me and this is my car." She hoped he was Mr. Angus. She didn't like his name and since she was to see Mr. Brown first, she hoped he was the more flatteringly portrayed.

The door to the cubby hole opened and the girl Mr. Brown had called Grace, came out. The expression on her face was too business-like to be natural. It seemed as if it had been placed there for a purpose.

She walked toward Emma Lou, who got up and stood like a child, waiting for punishment and hoping all the while that it will dissipate itself in threats. The typewriter was stilled and Emma Lou could feel an extra pair of eyes looking at her. The girl drew close, then spoke:

"I'm sorry, Miss. Mr. Brown says he has some one else in view for the job. We'll call the agency. Thank you for coming in."

Thank her for coming in? What could she say? What should she say? The girl was smiling at her, but Emma Lou noticed that her fair skin was flushed and that her eyes danced nervously. Could she be hoping that Emma Lou would hurry and depart? The door was near. It opened easily. The steps were steep. One went down slowly. Seventh Avenue was still spangled with fore-noon sunshine and shadow. Its pavement was hard and hot. The windows in the buildings facing it, gleaming reflectors of the mounting sun.

Emma Lou returned to the employment agency. It was still crowded and more stuffy than ever. The sun had advanced high into the sky and it seemed to be centering its rays on that solitary defenseless window. There was still much conversation. There were still people crowded around the desk, still people in all the chairs, people and talk and heat and smells.

"Mrs. Blake is waiting for you," the gray-haired lady with the young face was unflustered and cool. Emma Lou went into the inner office. Mrs. Blake looked up quickly and forced a smile. The good-looking young man, more than ever resembling a Y.M.C.A. secretary, turned his back and fumbled with the card files. Mrs. Blake suggested that he leave the room. He did, beaming benevolently at Emma Lou as he went.

"I'm sorry," Mrs. Blake was very kind and womanly. "Mr. Brown called me. I didn't know he had some one else in mind. He hadn't told me."

"That's all right," replied Emma Lou briskly. "Have you something else?"

"Not now. Er-er. Have you had luncheon? It's early yet, I

know, but I generally go about this time. Come along, won't
you, I'd like to talk to you. I'll be ready in about thirty minutes
if you don't mind the wait."

Emma Lou warmed to the idea. At that moment, she would
have warmed toward any suggestion of friendliness. Here, perhaps, was a chance to make a welcome contact. She was lonesome and disappointed, so she readily assented and felt elated
and superior as she walked out of the office with the "boss."

They went to Eddie's for luncheon. Eddie's was an elbow-
shaped combination lunch-counter and dining room that
embraced a United Cigar Store on the northeast corner of 135th
Street and Seventh Avenue. Following Mrs. Blake's lead, Emma
Lou ordered a full noontime dinner, and, flattered by Mrs.
Blake's interest and congeniality, began to talk about herself.
She told of her birthplace and her home life. She told of her
high school days, spoke proudly of the fact that she had been the
only Negro student and how she had graduated cum laude.
Asked about her college years, she talked less freely. Mrs. Blake
sensed a cue.

"Didn't you like college?"

"For a little while, yes."

"What made you dislike it? Surely not the studies?"

"No." She didn't care to discuss this. "I was lonesome, I
guess."

"Weren't there any other colored boys and girls? I
thought . . ."

Emma Lou spoke curtly. "Oh, yes, quite a number, but I suppose I didn't mix well."

The waiter came to take the order for dessert, and Emma
Lou seized upon the fact that Mrs. Blake ordered sliced oranges
to talk about California's orange groves, California's sunshine—
anything but the California college she had attended and from
which she had fled. In vain did Mrs. Blake try to maneuver the
conversation back to Emma Lou's college experiences. She
would have none of it and Mrs. Blake was finally forced to give
it up.

When they were finished, Mrs. Blake insisted upon taking the
check. This done, she began to talk about jobs.

"You know, Miss Morgan, good jobs are rare. It is seldom I have anything to offer outside of the domestic field. Most Negro business offices are family affairs. They either get their help from within their own family group or from among their friends. Then, too," Emma Lou noticed that Mrs. Blake did not look directly at her, "lots of our Negro business men have a definite type of girl in mind and will not hire any other."

Emma Lou wondered what it was Mrs. Blake seemed to be holding back. She began again:

"My advice to you is that you enter Teachers' College and if you *will* stay in New York, get a job in the public school system. You can easily take a light job of some kind to support you through your course. Maybe with three years' college you won't need to go to training school. Why don't you find out about that? Now, if I were you. . . ." Mrs. Blake talked on, putting much emphasis on every "If I were you."

Emma Lou grew listless and antagonistic. She didn't like this little sawed-off woman as she was now, being business-like and giving advice. She was glad when they finally left Eddie's, and more than glad to escape after having been admonished not to over-sleep, "But be in my office, and I'll see what I can do for you, dearie, early in the morning. There's sure to be something."

Left to herself, Emma Lou strolled south on the west side of Seventh Avenue to 134th Street, then crossed over to the east side and turned north. She didn't know what to do. It was too late to consider visiting another employment agency, and, furthermore, she didn't have enough money left to pay another fee. Let jobs go until tomorrow, then she would return to Mrs. Blake's, ask for a return of her fee, and find some other employment agency, a more imposing one, if possible. She had had enough of those on 135th Street.

She didn't want to go home, either. Her room had no outside vista. If she sat in the solitary chair by the solitary window, all she could see were other windows and brick walls and people either mysteriously or brazenly moving about in the apartments across the court. There was no privacy there, little fresh air, and no natural light after the sun began its downward course. Then

the apartment always smelled of frying fish or of boiling cabbage. Her landlady seemed to alternate daily between these two
foods. Fish smells and cabbage smells pervaded the long, dark
hallway, swirled into the room when the door was opened, and
perfumed one's clothes disagreeably. Moreover, urinal and fecal
smells surged upward from the garbage-littered bottom of the
court which her window faced.

If she went home, the landlady would eye her suspiciously
and ask, "Ain't you got a job yet?" then move away, shaking her
head and dipping into her snuff box. Occasionally, in moments
of excitement, she spat on the floor. And the little fat man who
had the room next to Emma Lou's could be heard coughing
suggestively—tapping on the wall, and talking to himself in
terms of her. He had seen her slip John in last night. He might
be more bold now. He might even try—oh no he wouldn't.

She was crossing 137th Street. She remembered this corner.
John had told her that he could always be found there after work
any spring or summer evening.

Emma Lou had met John on her first day in New York. He
was employed as a porter in the theater where Mazelle Lindsay
was scheduled to perform, and, seeing a new maid on the prem-
ises, had decided to "make" her. He had. Emma Lou had not
liked him particularly, but he had seemed New Yorkish and
genial. It was John who had found her her room. It was John
who had taught her how to find her way up and down town on
the subway and on the elevated. He had also conducted her on
a Cook's tour of Harlem, had strolled up and down Seventh
Avenue with her evenings after they had come uptown from the
theater. He had pointed out for her the Y.W.C.A. with its
imposing annex, the Emma Ranson House, and suggested that
she get a room there later on. He had taken her on a Sunday to
several of the Harlem motion picture and vaudeville theaters,
and he had been as painstaking in pointing out the churches as
he had been lax in pointing out the cabarets. Moreover, as they
strolled Seventh Avenue, he had attempted to give her all the
"inside dope" on Harlem, had told her of the "rent parties," of
the "numbers," of "hot" men, of "sweetbacks," and other local
phenomena.

Emma Lou was now passing a barber shop near 140th Street.
A group of men were standing there beneath a huge white and
black sign announcing, "Bobbing's, fifty cents; haircuts, twenty-
five cents." They were whistling at three school girls, about
fourteen or fifteen years of age, who were passing, doing much
switching and giggling. Emma Lou curled her lips. Harlem
streets presented many such scenes. She looked at the men sig-
nificantly, forgetting for the moment that it was none of her
business what they or the girls did. But they didn't notice her.
They were too busy having fun with those fresh little chippies.

Emma Lou experienced a feeling of resentment, then, realizing how ridiculous it all was, smiled it away and began to think
of John once more. She wondered why she had submitted herself to him. Was it cold-blooded payment for his kind chaperon-
ing? Something like that. John wasn't her type. He was too
pudgy and dark, too obviously an ex-cotton-picker from Georgia.
He was unlettered and she couldn't stand for that, for she liked
intelligent-looking, slender, light-brown-skinned men, like, well
. . . like the one who was just passing. She admired him boldly.
He looked at her, then over her, and passed on.

Seventh Avenue was becoming more crowded now. School
children were out for their lunch hour, corner loafers and pool-
hall loiterers were beginning to collect on their chosen spots.
Knots of people, of no particular designation, also stood around
talking, or just looking, and there were many pedestrians, either
impressing one as being in a great hurry, or else seeming to have
no place at all to go. Emma Lou was in this latter class. By now
she had reached 142nd Street and had decided to cross over to
the opposite side and walk south once more. Seventh Avenue
was a wide, well-paved, busy thoroughfare, with a long, narrow,
iron fenced-in parkway dividing the east side from the west.
Emma Lou liked Seventh Avenue. It was so active and alive, so
different from Central Avenue, the dingy main street of the
black belt of Los Angeles. At night it was glorious! Where else
could one see so many different types of Negroes? Where else
would one view such a heterogeneous ensemble of mellow colors, glorified by the night?

People passing by. Children playing. Dogs on leashes. Stray

cats crouching by the sides of buildings. Men standing in groups
or alone. Black men. Yellow men. Brown men. Emma Lou eyed
them. They eyed her. There were a few remarks passed. She
thought she got their import even though she could not hear
what they were saying. She quickened her step and held her
head higher. Be yourself, Emma Lou. Do you want to start pick-
ing men up off the street?

The heat became more intense. Brisk walking made her per-
spire. Her underclothes grew sticky. Harlem heat was so muggy.
She could feel the shine on her nose and it made her self-
conscious. She remembered how the "Grace" in the office of
Angus and Brown had so carefully powdered her skin before
confronting her employer, and, as she remembered this, she
looked up, and sure enough, here she was in front of the building she had sought so eagerly earlier that morning. Emma Lou
drew closer to the building. She must get that shine off her nose.
It was bad enough to be black, too black, without having a shiny
face to boot. She stepped in front of the tailor shop directly
beneath the office of Angus and Brown, and, turning her back
to the street, proceeded to powder her shiny member. Three
noisy lads passed by. They saw Emma Lou and her reflection in
the sunlit show window. The one closest to her cleared his
throat and crooned out, loud enough for her to hear, "There's a
girl for you 'Fats.'" "Fats" was the one in the middle. He had a
rotund form and a coffee-colored face. He was in his shirt
sleeves and carried his coat on his arm. Bell-bottom trousers hid
all save the tips of his shiny tan shoes. "Fats" was looking at
Emma Lou, too, but as he passed, he turned his eyes from her
and broadcast a withering look at the lad who had spoken:

"Man, you know I don't haul no coal." There was loud laughter and the trio merrily clicked their metal-cornered heels on
the sun-baked pavement as they moved away.

Part 3

Alva

It was nine o'clock. The alarm rang. Alva's roommate awoke cursing.

"Why the hell don't you turn off that alarm?"

There was no response. The alarm continued to ring.

"Alva," Braxton yelled into his sleeping roommate's ear. "Turn off that clock. Wake up," he began shaking him, "Wake up, damn you . . . ya dead?"

Alva slowly emerged from his stupor. Almost mechanically he reached for the clock, dancing merrily on a chair close to the bed, and, finding it, pushed the guilty lever back into the silent zone. Braxton watched him disgustedly:

"Watcha gettin' up so early for? Don'tcha know this is Monday?"

"Sure, I know it's Monday, but I gotta go to Uncle's. The landlord'll be here before eleven o'clock."

"Watcha gonna pawn?"

"My brown suit. I won't need it 'til next Sunday. You got your rent?"

"I got four dollars," Braxton advanced slowly.

"Cantcha get the other two?"

Braxton grew apologetic and explanatory. "Not today . . . ya . . . see . . ."

"Aw, man, you make me sick."

Disgust overcoming his languor, Alva got out of the bed. This was getting to be a regular Monday morning occurrence.

Braxton was always one, two, or three dollars short of having his required half of the rent, and Alva, who had rented the room, always had to make it up. Luckily for Alva, both he and the land-lord were Elks. Fraternal brothers must stick together. Thus it was an easy matter to pay the rent in installments. The only dif-ficulty being that it was happening rather frequently. There is liable to be a limit even to a brother Elk's patience, especially where money is concerned.

Alva put on his dressing gown, and his house shoes, then went into the little alcove which was curtained off in the rear from the rest of the room. Jumbled together on the marble-topped sta-tionary washstand were a half dozen empty gin bottles bearing a pre-prohibition Gordon label, a similar number of empty gin-ger ale bottles, a cocktail shaker, and a medley of assorted cock-tail, water, jelly, and whiskey glasses, filled and surrounded by squeezed orange and lemon rinds. The little two-burner gas plate atop a wooden dry-goods box was covered with dirty dishes, frying pan, egg shells, bacon rinds, and a dominating though lopsided tea kettle. Even Alva's trunk, which occupied half the entrance space between the alcove and the room, lit-tered as it was with paper bags, cracker boxes, and greasy paper plates, bore evidence of the orgy which the occupants of the room staged over every weekend.

Alva surveyed this rather intimate and familiar disorder, fal-tered a moment, started to call Braxton, then remembering pre-vious Monday mornings set about his task alone. It was Braxton's custom never to arise before noon. Alva, who worked as a press-er in a costume house, was forced to get up at seven o'clock on every week day save Monday when he was not required to report for work until twelve o'clock. His employers thus managed to accumulate several baskets of clothes from the sewing room before their pressers arrived. It was better to have then remain at home until this was done. Then you didn't have to pay them so much, and having let the sewing room get a head start, there was never any chance for the pressing room to slow down.

Alva's mother had been an American mulatto, his father a Filipino. Alva himself was small in stature as his father had been, small and well developed with broad shoulders, narrow hips, and firm, well-modeled limbs. His face was oval-shaped and his features more oriental than Negroid. His skin was neither yellow nor brown but something in between, something warm, arresting, and mellow with the faintest suggestion of a parchment tinge beneath, lending it individuality. His eyes were small, deep, and slanting. His forehead high, hair sparse and finely textured.

The alcove finally straightened up, Alva dressed rather hurriedly, and, taking a brown suit from the closet, made his regular Monday morning trip to the pawn shop.

Emma Lou finished rinsing out some silk stockings and sat down in a chair to re-read a letter she had received from home that morning. It was about the third time she had gone over it. Her mother wanted her to come home. Evidently the hometown gossips were busy. No doubt they were saying, "Strange mother to let that gal stay in New York alone. She ain't goin' to school, either. Wonder what she's doin'?" Emma Lou read all this between the lines of what her mother had written. Jane Morgan was being tearful as usual. She loved to suffer, and being tearful seemed the easiest way to let the world know that one was suffering. Sob stuff, thought Emma Lou, and, tearing the letter up, threw it into the waste paper basket.

Emma Lou was now maid to Arline Strange, who was playing for the moment the part of a mulatto Carmen in an alleged melodrama of Negro life in Harlem. Having tried, for two weeks, to locate what she termed "congenial work," Emma Lou had given up the idea and meekly returned to Mazelle Lindsay. She had found her old job satisfactorily filled, but Mazelle had been sympathetic and had arranged to place her with Arline Strange. Now her mother wanted her to come home. Let her want. She was of age, and supporting herself. Moreover, she felt that if it had not been for gossip her mother would never have thought of asking her to come home.

"Stop your mooning, dearie." Arline Strange had returned to her dressing room. Act One was over. The Negro Carmen had become the mistress of a wealthy European. She would now shed her gingham dress for an evening gown.

Mechanically, Emma Lou assisted Arline in making the change. She was unusually silent. It was noticed.

"'Smatter, Louie. In love or something?"

Emma Lou smiled, "Only with myself."

"Then snap out of it. Remember you're going cabareting with us tonight. This brother of mine from Chicago insists upon going to Harlem to check up on my performance. He'll enjoy himself more if you act as guide. Ever been to Small's?" Emma Lou shook her head. "I haven't been to any of the cabarets."

"What?" Arline was genuinely surprised. "You in Harlem and never been to a cabaret? Why I thought all colored people went."

Emma Lou bristled. White people were so stupid. "No," she said firmly. "All colored people don't go. Fact is, I've heard most of the places are patronized almost solely by whites."

"Oh, yes, I knew that, I've been to Small's and Barron's and the Cotton Club, but I thought there were other places." She stopped talking, and spent the next few moments deepening the artificial duskiness of her skin. The gingham dress was now on its hanger. The evening gown clung glamorously to her voluptuous figure. "For God's sake, don't let on to my brother you ain't been to Small's before. Act like you know all about it. I'll see that he gives you a big tip." The call bell rang. Arline said "Damn," gave one last look in the mirror, then hurried back to the stage so that the curtain could go up on the cabaret scene in Act Two.

Emma Lou laid out the negligee outfit Arline would be killed in at the end of Act Three, and went downstairs to stand in the stage wings, a makeup box beneath her arm. She never tired of watching the so-called dramatic antics on the stage. She wondered if there were any Negroes of the type portrayed by Arline and her fellow performers. Perhaps there were, since there were any number of minor parts being played by real Negroes who acted much different from any Negroes she had ever known or seen. It all seemed to her like a mad caricature.

She watched for about the thirtieth time Arline acting the part of a Negro cabaret entertainer, and also for about the thirtieth time, came to the conclusion that Arline was being herself rather than the character she was supposed to be playing. From where she was standing in the wings she could see a small portion of the audience, and she watched their reaction. Their interest seemed genuine. Arline did have pep and personality, and the alleged Negro background was strident and kaleidoscopic, all of which no doubt made up for the inane plot and vulgar dialogue.

They entered Small's Paradise, Emma Lou, Arline, and Arline's brother from Chicago. All the way uptown he had plied Emma Lou with questions concerning New York's Black Belt. He had reciprocated by relating how well he knew the Negro section of Chicago. Quite a personage around the Black and Tan cabarets there, it seemed. "But I never," he concluded as the taxi drew up to the curb in front of Small's, "have seen any black gal in Chicago act like Arline acts. She claims she is presenting a Harlem specie. So I am going to see for myself." And he chuckled all the time he was helping them out of the taxi and paying the fare. While they were checking their wraps in the foyer, the orchestra began playing. Through the open entrance way Emma Lou could see a hazy, dim-lighted room, walls and ceiling colorfully decorated, floor space jammed with tables and chairs and people. A heavy-set mulatto in tuxedo, after asking how many were in their party, led them through a lane of tables around the squared-off dance platform to a ringside seat on the far side of the cabaret.

Immediately they were seated, a waiter came to take their order.

"Three bottles of White Rock." The waiter nodded, twirled his tray on the tip of his fingers and skated away.

Emma Lou watched the dancers, and noticed immediately that in all that insensate crowd of dancing couples there were only a few Negroes.

"My God, such music. Let's dance, Arline," and off they went, leaving Emma Lou sitting alone. Somehow or other she felt frightened. Most of the tables around her were deserted, their tops littered with liquid-filled glasses, and bottles of ginger ale and White Rock. There was no liquor in sight, yet Emma Lou was aware of pungent alcoholic odors. Then she noticed a heavy-jowled white man with a flashlight walking among the empty tables and looking beneath them. He didn't seem to be finding anything. The music soon stopped. Arline and her brother returned to the table. He was feigning anxiety because he had not seen the type of character Arline claimed to be portraying, and loudly declared that he was disappointed.

"Why there ain't nothing here but white people. Is it always like this?"

Emma Lou said that it was and turned to watch their waiter, who with two others had come dancing across the floor, holding aloft his tray, filled with bottles and glasses. Deftly, he maneuvered away from the other two and slid to their table, put down a bottle of White Rock and an ice-filled glass before each one, then, after flicking a stub check on to the table, rejoined his companions in a return trip across the dance floor.

Arline's brother produced a hip flask, and before Emma Lou could demur mixed her a highball. She didn't want to drink. She hadn't drunk before, but. . . .

"Here come the entertainers!" Emma Lou followed Arline's turn of the head to see two women, one light-brown skin and slim, the other chocolate-colored and fat, walking to the center of the dance floor.

The orchestra played the introduction and vamp to "Muddy Waters." The two entertainers swung their legs and arms in rhythmic unison, smiling broadly and rolling their eyes, first to the left and then to the right. Then they began to sing. Their voices were husky and strident, neither alto nor soprano. They muddled their words and seemed to impregnate the syncopated melody with physical content.

As they sang the chorus, they glided out among the tables, stopping at one, then at another, and another, singing all the time, their bodies undulating and provocative, occasionally giving just a promise of an obscene hip movement, while their arms waved and their fingers held tight to the dollar bills and silver coins placed in their palms by enthusiastic onlookers.

Emma Lou, all of her, watched and listened. As they approached her table, she sat as one mesmerized. Something in her seemed to be trying to give way. Her insides were stirred, and tingled. The two entertainers circled their table; Arline's brother held out a dollar bill. The fat, chocolate-colored girl leaned over the table, her hand touched his, she exercised the muscles of her stomach, muttered a guttural "Thank you" in between notes and moved away, moaning "Muddy Waters," rolling her eyes, shaking her hips.

Emma Lou had turned completely around in her chair, watching the progress of that wah-wahing, jello-like chocolate hulk, and her slim, light-brown-skin companion. Finally they completed their rounds of the tables and returned to the dance floor. Red and blue spotlights played upon their dissimilar fig-ures, the orchestra increased the tempo and lessened the inten-sity of its playing. They swaying entertainers pulled up their dresses, exposing lace trimmed stepins and an island of flesh. Their stockings were rolled down below their knees, their ste-pins discreetly short and delicate. Finally, they ceased their swaying and began to dance. They shimmied and whirled, charlestoned and black-bottomed. Their terpsichorean ensem-ble was melodramatic and absurd. Their execution easy and emphatic. Emma Lou forgot herself. She gaped, giggled and applauded like the rest of the audience, and only as they let their legs separate, preparatory to doing one final split to the floor, did Emma Lou come to herself long enough to wonder if the fat one could achieve it without seriously endangering those ever tightening stepins.

"Dam' good, I'll say," a slender white youth at the next table asseverated, as he lifted an amber-filled glass to his lips.

Arline sighed. Her brother had begun to razz her. Emma Lou blinked guiltily as the lights were turned up. She had been immersed in something disturbingly pleasant. Idiot, she berated herself, just because you've had one drink and seen your first cabaret entertainer, must your mind and body feel all aflame?

Arline's brother was mixing another highball. All around, people were laughing. There was much more laughter than there was talk, much more gesticulating and ogling than the usual means of expression called for. Everything seemed unre-strained, abandoned. Yet, Emma Lou was conscious of a note of artificiality, the same as she felt when she watched Arline and her fellow performers cavorting on the stage in "Cabaret Gal." This entire scene seemed staged, they were in a theater, only the proscenium arch had been obliterated. At last the audience and the actors were as one.

A call to order on the snare drum. A brutal sliding trumpet call on the trombone, a running minor scale by the clarinet and piano, and umpah, umpah by the bass horn, a combination four-measure moan and strum by the saxophone and banjo, then a melodic ensemble, and the orchestra was playing another dance tune. Masses of people jumbled up the three entrances to the dance square and with difficulty, singled out their mates and became closely allied partners. Inadvertently, Emma Lou looked at Arline's brother. He blushed, and appeared uncomfortable. She realized immediately what was on his mind. He didn't know whether or not to ask her to dance with him. The ethics of the case were complex. She was a Negro and hired maid. But was she a hired maid after hours, and in this environment? Emma Lou had difficulty in suppressing a smile, then she decided to end the suspense.

"Why don't you two dance. No need of letting the music go to waste."

Both Arline and her brother were obviously relieved, but as they got up Arline said, "Ain't much fun cuddling up to your own brother when there's music like this." But off they went, leaving Emma Lou alone and disturbed. John ought to be here, slipped out before she remembered that she didn't want John any more. Then she began to wish that John had introduced her to some more men. But he didn't know the kind of men she was interested in knowing. He only knew men and boys like himself, porters and janitors and chauffeurs and bootblacks. Imagine her, a college-trained person, even if she hadn't finished her senior year, being satisfied with the company of such unintelligent servitors. How had she stood John for so long with his constant defense, "I ain't got much education, but I got mother wit." Mother wit. Creation of the unlettered, satisfying illusion to the dumb, ludicrous prop to the mentally unfit. Yes, he had mother wit all right.

Emma Lou looked around and noticed at a nearby table three

young colored men, all in tuxedos, gazing at her and talking. She
averted her glance and turned to watch the dancers. She thought
she heard a burst of ribald laughter from the young men at the
table. Then some one touched her on the shoulder, and she
looked up into a smiling oriental-like face, neither brown nor
yellow in color, but warm and pleasing beneath the soft lights,
and, because of the smile, showing a gleaming row of small,
even teeth, set off by a solitary gold incisor. The voice was per-
suasive and apologetic, "Would you care to dance with me?"
The music had stopped, but there was promise of an encore.
Emma Lou was confused, her mind blankly chaotic. She was
expected to push back her chair and get up. She did. And, without saying a word, allowed herself to be maneuvered to the
dance floor.

In a moment they were swallowed up in the jazz whirlpool.
Long strides were impossible. There were too many other legs
striding for free motion in that overpopulated area. He held her
close to him; the contours of her body fitting his. The two high-
balls had made her giddy. She seemed to be glowing inside. The
soft lights and the music suggested abandon and intrigue. They
said nothing to one another. She noticed that her partner's face
seemed alive with some inner ecstasy. It must be the music,
thought Emma Lou. Then she got a whiff of his liquor-laden
breath.

After three encores, the clarinet shrilled out a combination of
notes that seemed to say regretfully, "That's all." Brighter lights
were switched on, and the milling couples merged into a struggling mass of individuals, laughing, talking, overanimated individuals, all trying to go in different directions, and getting a
great deal of fun out of the resulting confusion. Emma Lou's
partner held tightly to her arm, and pushed her through the
insensate crowd to her table. Then he muttered a polite "thank
you" and turned away. Emma Lou sat down. Arline and her
brother looked at her and laughed. "Got a dance, eh Louie?"
Emma Lou wondered if Arline was being malicious, and for an
answer she only nodded her head and smiled, hoping all the
while that her smile was properly enigmatic.

Arline's brother spoke up. "Whadda say we go. I've seen

enough of this to know that Arline and her stage director are all wet." Their waiter was called, the check was paid, and they were on their way out. In spite of herself, Emma Lou glanced back to the table where her dancing partner was sitting. To her confusion, she noticed that he and his two friends were staring at her. One of them said something and made a wry face. Then they all laughed, uproariously and cruelly.

Alva had overslept. Braxton, who had stayed out the entire night, came in about eight o'clock, and excitedly interrupted his drunken slumber.

"Ain't you goin' to work?"

"Work?" Alva was alarmed. "What time is it?"

"'Bout eight. Didn't you set the clock?"

"Sure, I did." Alva picked up the clock from the floor and examined the alarm dial. It had been set for ten o'clock instead of for six. He sulked for a moment, then attempted to shake off the impending mood of regretfulness and disgust for self.

"Ah, hell, what's the dif'. Call 'em up and tell 'em I'm sick. There's a nickel somewhere in that change on the dresser." Braxton had taken off his tuxedo coat and vest.

"If you're not goin' to work ever, you might as well quit. I don't see no sense in working two days and laying off three."

"I'm goin' to quit the damn job anyway. I been working steady now since last fall."

"I thought it was about time you quit." Braxton had stripped off his white full-dress shirt, put on his bathrobe, and started out of the room, to go downstairs to the telephone. Alva reached across the bed and pulled up the shade, blinked at the inpouring daylight and lay himself back down, one arm thrown across his forehead. He had slipped off into a state of semi-consciousness again when Braxton returned.

"The girl said she'd tell the boss. Asked who I was as usual." He went into the alcove to finish undressing, and put on his pajamas. Alva looked up.

"You goin' to bed?"

"Yes, don't you think I want some sleep?"

"Thought you was goin' to look for a job?"

"I was, but I hadn't figured on staying out all night."

"Always some damn excuse. Where'd you go?"

"Down to Flo's."

"Who in the hell is Flo?"

"That little yaller broad I picked up at the cabaret last night."

"I thought she had a nigger with her."

"She did, but I jived her along, so she ditched him, and gave me her address. I met her there later."

Braxton was now ready to get into the bed. All this time he had been preparing himself in his usual bedtime manner. His face had been cold-creamed, his hair greased and covered by a silken stocking cap. This done, he climbed over Alva and lay on top of the covers. They were silent for a moment, then Braxton laughed softly to himself.

"Where'd *you* go last night?"

"Where'd I go?" Alva seemed surprised. "Why I came home, where'd ya think I went?" Braxton laughed again.

"Oh, I thought maybe you'd really made a date with that coal scuttle blond you danced with."

"Ya musta thought it."

"Well, ya seemed pretty sweet on her."

"Whaddaya mean, sweet? Just because I danced with her once. I took pity on her, 'cause she looked so lonesome with those ofays. Wonder who they was?"

"Oh, she probably works for them. It's good you danced with her. Nobody else would."

"I didn't see nothing wrong with her. She might have been a little dark."

"Little dark is right, and you know when they comes blacker'n me, they ain't got no go." Braxton was a reddish brown aristocrat, with clear-cut features and curly hair. His paternal grandfather had been an Iroquois Indian.

Emma Lou was very lonesome. She still knew no one save John, two or three of the Negro actors who worked on the stage with Arline, and a West Indian woman who lived in the same apartment with her. Occasionally John met her when she left the theater at night and escorted her to her apartment door. He repeatedly importuned her to be nice to him once more. Her answer only was a sigh or a smile.

The West Indian woman was employed as a stenographer in the office of a Harlem political sheet. She was shy and retiring, and not much given to making friends with American Negroes. So many of them had snubbed and pained her when she was newly emigrant from her home in Barbados, that she lumped them all together, just as they seemed to do her people. She would not take under consideration that Emma Lou was new to Harlem, and not even aware of the prejudice American-born Harlemites nursed for foreign-born ones. She remembered too vividly how, on ringing the bell of a house where there had been a vacancy sign in the window, a little girl had come to the door, and, in answer to a voice in the back asking, "Who is it, Cora?" had replied, "monkey chaser wants to see the room you got to rent." Jasmine Griffith was wary of all contact with American Negroes, for that had been only one of the many embittering incidents she had experienced.

Emma Lou liked Jasmine, but was conscious of the fact that she could never penetrate her stolid reserve. They often talked to one another when they met in the hallway, and sometimes they stopped in one another's rooms, but there was never any talk of going places together, never any informal revelations or intimacies.

The Negro actors in "Cabaret Gal" all felt themselves superior to Emma Lou, and she in turn felt superior to them. She was just a maid. They were just common stage folk. Once she had had an inspiration. She had heard that "Cabaret Gal" was liable to run for two years or more on Broadway before road shows were sent out. Without saying anything to Arline she had approached the stage director and asked him, in all secrecy, what her chances were of getting into the cabaret ensemble. She knew they paid well, and she speculated that two or three years in "Cabaret Gal" might lay the foundations for a future stage career.

"What the hell would Arline do," he laughed, "if she didn't have you to change her complexion before every performance?"

Emma Lou had smiled away this bit of persiflage and had reiterated her request in such a way that there was no mistaking her seriousness.

Sensing this, the director changed his mood, and admitted that even then two of the girls were dropping out of "Cabaret Gal" to sail for Europe with another show, booked for a season on the continent. But he hastened to tell her, as he saw her eyes brighten with anticipation:

"Well, you see, we worked out a color scheme that would be a complement to Arline's makeup. You've noticed, no doubt, that all the girls are about one color, and . . ."

Unable to stammer any more, he had hastened away, embarrassed.

Emma Lou hadn't noticed that all the girls were one color. In fact, she was certain they were not. She hastened to stand in the stage wings among them between scenes and observe their skin coloring. Despite many layers of liquid powder she could see that they were not all one color, but that they were either mulatto or light-brown skin. Their makeup and the lights gave them an appearance of sameness. She noticed that there were several black men in the ensemble, but that none of the women were dark. Then the breach between Emma Lou and the show people widened.

Emma Lou had another inspiration. She had decided to move. Perhaps if she were to live with a homey type of family they could introduce her to "the right sort of people." She blamed her enforced isolation on the fact that she had made no worthwhile contacts. Mrs. Blake was a disagreeable remembrance. Since she came to think about it, Mrs. Blake had been distinctly patronizing like . . . like . . . her high school principal, or like Doris Garrett, the head of the only Negro sorority in the Southern California college she had attended. Doris Garrett had been very nice to all her colored schoolmates, but had seen to it that only those girls who were of a mulatto type were pledged for membership in the Green letter society of which she was the head.

Emma Lou reasoned that she couldn't go on as she was, being alone and aching for congenial companionship. True, her job didn't allow her much spare time. She had to be at Arline's apartment at eleven every morning, but except on two matinee days, she was free from two until seven-thirty P.M., when she had to be at the theater, and by eleven-thirty every night, she was in Harlem. Then she had all day Sunday to herself. Arline paid her a good salary, and she made tips from the first and second leads in the show, who used her spare moments. She had been working for six weeks now, and had saved one hundred dollars. She practically lived on her tips. Her salary was twenty-five dollars per week. Dinner was the only meal she had to pay for, and Arline gave her many clothes.

So Emma Lou began to think seriously of getting another room. She wanted more space and more air and more freedom from fish and cabbage smells. She had been in Harlem now for about fourteen weeks. Only fourteen weeks? The count stunned her. It seemed much longer. It was this rut she was in. Well, she would get out of it. Finding a room, a new room, would be the first step.

Emma Lou asked Jasmine how one went about it. Jasmine was noncommittal and said she didn't know, but she had heard that *The Amsterdam News*, a Harlem Negro weekly, carried a large "Furnished rooms for rent" section. Emma Lou bought a copy of this paper, and, though attracted, did not stop to read the news columns under the streaming headlines to the effect "Headless Man Found In Trunk"; "Number Runner Given Sentence"; "Benefit Ball Huge Success"; but turned immediately to the advertising section.

There were many rooms advertised for rent, rooms of all sizes and for all prices, with all sorts of conveniences and inconveniences. Emma Lou was more bewildered than ever. Then, remembering that John had said that all the "dictys" lived between Seventh and Edgecombe Avenues on 136th, 137th, 138th, and 139th Streets, decided to check off the places in these streets. John had also told her that "dictys" lived in the imposing apartment houses on Edgecombe, Bradhurst, and St. Nicholas Avenues. "Dictys" were Harlem's high-toned people, folk listed in the local social register, as it were. But Emma Lou did not care to live in another apartment building. She pre-

ferred, or thought she would prefer, living in a private house
where there would be fewer people and more privacy.

The first place Emma Lou approached had a double room for
two girls, two men, or a couple. They thought their advertise-
ment had said as much. It hadn't, but Emma Lou apologized,
and left. The next three places were nice but exorbitant. Front
rooms with two windows and a kitchenette, renting for twelve,
fourteen, and sixteen dollars a week. Emma Lou had planned to
spend not more than eight or nine dollars at the most. The next
place smelled far worse than her present home. The room was
smaller and the rent higher. Emma Lou began to lose hope,
then rallying, had gone to the last place on her list from *The
Amsterdam News*. The landlady was the spinster type, garrulous
and friendly. She had a high forehead, keen intellectual eyes,
and a sharp profile. The room she showed to Emma Lou was
both spacious and clean, and she only asked eight dollars and
fifty cents per week for it.

After showing her the room, the landlady had invited Emma
Lou downstairs to her parlor. Emma Lou found a place to sit
down on a damask-covered divan. There were many other seats
in the room, but the landlady, *Miss* Carrington, as she had introduced herself, insisted upon sitting down beside her. They
talked for about a half an hour, and in that time, being a successful "pumper," *Miss* Carrington had learned the history of Emma
Lou's experiences in Harlem. Satisfied of her ground, she grew
more familiar, placed her hand on Emma Lou's knee, then
finally put her arm around her waist. Emma Lou felt uncomfortable. This sudden and unexpected intimacy disturbed her.
The room was close and hot. Damask coverings seemed to be
everywhere. Damask coverings and dull red draperies and
mauve walls.

"Don't worry any more, dearie, I'll take care of you from now
on," and she had tightened her arm around Emma Lou's waist,
who, feeling more uncomfortable than ever, looked at her wrist
watch.

"I must be going."

"Do you want the room?" There was a note of anxiety in her
voice. "There are lots of nice girls living here. We call this the

'Old Maid's Home.' We have parties among ourselves, and just
have a grand time. Talk about fun! I know you'd be happy
here."

Emma Lou knew she would, too, and said as much. Then
hastily, she gave *Miss* Carrington a three dollar deposit on the
room, and left . . . to continue her search for a new place to
live.

There were no more places on her *Amsterdam News* list, so
noticing "Vacancy" signs in windows along the various streets,
Emma Lou decided to walk along and blindly choose a house.
None of the houses in 137th Street impressed her, they were all
too cold-looking, and she was through with 136th Street. *Miss*
Carrington lived there. She sauntered down the "L" trestled
Eighth Avenue to 138th Street. Then she turned toward Seventh
Avenue and strolled along slowly on the south side of the street.
She chose the south side because she preferred the appearance
of the red-brick houses there to the green-brick ones on the
north side. After she had passed by three "Vacancy" signs, she
decided to enter the very next house where such a sign was dis-
played.

Seeing one, she climbed the terraced stone stairs, rang the
doorbell, and waited expectantly. There was a long pause. She
rang the bell again, and just as she relieved her pressure, the
door was opened by a bedizened yellow woman with sand-
colored hair and deep-set corn-colored eyes. Emma Lou noted
the incongruous thickness of her lips.

"How do you do. I . . . I . . . would like to see one of your
rooms."

The woman eyed Emma Lou curiously and looked as if she
were about to snort. Then slowly she began to close the door in
the astonished girl's face. Emma Lou opened her mouth and
tried to speak but the woman forestalled her, saying testily in
broken English:

"We have nothing here."

Persons of color didn't associate with blacks in the Caribbean
Island she had come from.

From then on Emma Lou intensified her suffering, mulling
over and magnifying each malignant experience. They grew

within her and were nourished by constant introspection and livid reminiscences. Again, she stood upon the platform in the auditorium of the Boise high school. Again that first moment of realization and its attendant strictures were disinterred and revivified. She was black, too black, there was no getting around it. Her mother had thought so, and had often wished that she had been a boy. Black boys can make a go of it, but black girls . . .

No one liked black anyway. . . .

Wanted: light-colored girl to work as waitress in tearoom. . . .

Wanted: Nurse girl, light-colored preferred (children are afraid of black folks). . . .

"I don' haul no coal. . . ."

"It's like this, Emma Lou, they don't want no dark girls in their sorority. They ain't pledged us, and we're the only two they ain't, and we're both black."

The ineluctability of raw experience! The muddy mirroring of life's perplexities. . . . Seeing everything in terms of self. . . . The spreading sensitiveness of an adder's sting.

"Mr. Brown has some one else in mind. . . ."

"We have nothing here. . . ."

She should have been a boy. A black boy could get along, but a black girl. . . .

Arline was leaving the cast of "Cabaret Gal" for two weeks. Her mother had died in Chicago. The Negro Carmen must be played by an understudy, a real mulatto this time, who, lacking Arline's poise and personality, nevertheless brought down the house because of the crude vividity of her performance. Emma Lou was asked to act as her maid while Arline was away. Indignantly she had taken the alternative of a two weeks' vacation. Imagine her being maid for a *Negro* woman! It was unthinkable.

Left entirely to herself, she proceeded to make herself more miserable. Lying in bed late every morning, semi-conscious, body burning, mind disturbed by thoughts of sex. Never before had she experienced such physical longing. She often thought of

John and at times was almost driven to slip him into her room once more. But John couldn't satisfy her. She felt that she wanted something more than just the mere physical relationship with some one whose body and body coloring were distasteful to her.

When she did decide to get up, she would spend an hour before her dresser mirror, playing with her hair, parting it on the right side, then on the left, then in the middle, brushing it straight back, or else teasing it with the comb, inducing it to crackle with electric energy. Then she would cover it with a cap, pin a towel around her shoulders, and begin to experiment with her complexion.

She had decided to bleach her skin as much as possible. She had bought many creams and skin preparations, and had tried to remember the various bleaching aids she had heard of throughout her life. She remembered having heard her grandmother speak of that "old fool, Carrie Campbell," who, already a fair mulatto, had wished to pass for white. To accomplish this she had taken arsenic wafers, which were guaranteed to increase the pallor of one's skin.

Emma Lou had obtained some of these arsenic wafers and eaten them, but they had only served to give her pains in the pit of her stomach. Next she determined upon a peroxide solution in addition to something which was known as Black and White Ointment. After she had been using these for about a month she thought that she could notice some change. But in reality the only effects were an increase in blackheads, irritating rashes, and a burning skin.

Meanwhile she found her thoughts straying often to the chap she had danced with in the cabaret. She was certain he lived in Harlem, and she was determined to find him. She took it for granted that he would remember her. So day after day, she strolled up and down Seventh Avenue from 125th to 145th Street, then crossed to Lenox Avenue and traversed the same distance. *He* was her ideal. He looked like a college person. He dressed well. His skin was such a warm and different color, and she had been tantalized by the mysterious slant and deepness of his oriental-like eyes.

After walking the streets like this the first few days of her vacation, she became aware of the futility of her task. She saw many men on the street, many well-dressed, seemingly cultured, pleasingly colored men and boys. They seemed to congregate in certain places, and stand there all the day. She found herself wondering when and where they worked, and how they could afford to dress so well. She began to admire their well-formed bodies and gloried in the way their trousers fit their shapely limbs, and in the way they walked, bringing their heels down so firmly and so noisily on the pavement. Rubber heels were out of fashion. Hard heels with metal heel plates were the mode of the day. These corner loafers were so carefree, always smiling, eyes always bright. She loved to hear them laugh, and loved to watch them, when, without any seeming provocation, they would cut a few dance steps or do a jig. It seemed as if they either did this from sheer exuberance or else simply to relieve the monotony of standing still.

Of course, they noticed her as she passed and repassed day after day. She eyed them boldly enough, but she was still too self-conscious to broadcast an inviting look. She was too afraid of public ridicule or a mass mocking. Ofttimes men spoke to her, and tried to make advances, but they were never the kind she preferred. She didn't like black men, and the others seemed to keep their distance.

One day, tired of walking, she went into a motion picture theater on the avenue. She had seen the feature picture before, but was too lethargic and too uninterested in other things to go some place else. In truth, there was no place else for her to go. So she sat in the darkened theater, squirming around in her seat, and began to wonder just how many thousands of Negroes there were in Harlem. This theater was practically full, even in mid-afternoon. The streets were crowded, other theaters were crowded, and then there must be many more at home and at work. Emma Lou wondered what the population of Negro Harlem was. She should have read that Harlem number of the Survey Graphic issued two or three years ago. But Harlem hadn't interested her then for she had had no idea at the time that she would ever come to Harlem.

Some one sat down beside her. She was too occupied with herself to notice who the person was. The feature picture was over and a comedy was being flashed on the screen. Emma Lou found herself laughing, and, finding something on the screen to interest her, squared herself in her seat. Then she felt a pressure on one of her legs, the warm fleshy pressure of another leg. Her first impulse was to change her position. Perhaps she had touched the person next to her. Perhaps it was an accident. She moved her leg a little, but she still felt the pressure. Maybe it wasn't an accident. Her heart beat fast, her limbs began to quiver. The leg which was pressed against hers had such a pleasant, warm, fleshy feeling. She stole a glance at the person who had sat down next to her. He smiled . . . an impudent boyish smile and pressed the leg harder.

"Funny cuss, that guy," he was speaking to her.

Slap him in the face. Change your seat. Don't be an idiot. He has a nice smile. Look at him again.

"Did you see him in 'Long Pants'?"

He was leaning closer now, and Emma Lou took a note of a teakwood tan hand resting on her knee. She took another look at him, and saw that he had curly hair. He leaned toward her, and she leaned toward him. Their shoulders touched, his hand reached for hers and stole it from her lap. She wished that the theater wasn't so dark. But if it hadn't been so dark this couldn't have happened. She wondered if his hair and eyes were brown or jet black.

The feature picture was being reeled off again. They were too busy talking to notice that. When it was half over, they left their seats together. Before they reached the street, Emma Lou handed him three dollars, and, leaving the theater, they went to an apartment house on 140th Street, off Lenox Avenue. Emma Lou waited downstairs in the dirty marble hallway where she was stifled by urinal smells and stared at by passing people, waited for about ten minutes, then, in answer to his call, climbed one flight of stairs, and was led into a well-furnished, though dark, apartment.

His name was Jasper Crane. He was from Virginia. Living in Harlem with his brother, so he said. He had only been in New

York a month. Didn't have a job yet. His brother wasn't very nice to him . . . wanted to kick him out because he was jealous of him, thought his wife was more attentive than a sister-in-law should be. He asked Emma Lou to lend him five dollars. He said he wanted to buy a job. She did. And when he left her, he kissed her passionately and promised to meet her on the next day and to telephone her within an hour.

But he didn't telephone nor did Emma Lou ever see him again. Then she went to the motion picture theater where they had met, and sat in the same seat in the same row so that he could find her. She sat there through two shows, then came back on the next day, and on the next. Meanwhile several other men approached her, a panting fat Jew, whom she reported to the usher, a hunchback whom she pitied and then admired as he "made" the girl sitting on the other side of him; and there were several not very clean, trampy-looking men, but no Jasper.

He had asked her if she ever went to the Renaissance Casino, a public hall, where dances were held every night, so Emma Lou decided to go there on a Saturday, hoping to see him. She drew twenty-five dollars from the bank in order to buy a new dress, a very fine elaborate dress, which she got from a "hot" man, who had been recommended to her by Jasmine. "Hot" men sold supposedly stolen goods, thus enabling Harlem folk to dress well but cheaply. Then she spent the entire afternoon and evening preparing herself for the night, had her hair washed and marcelled, and her fingernails manicured.

Before putting on her dress she stood in front of her mirror for over an hour, fixing her face, drenching it with a peroxide solution, plastering it with a mudpack, massaging it with a bleaching ointment, and then, as a final touch, using much vanishing cream and powder. She even ate an arsenic wafer. The only visible effect of all this on her complexion was to give it an ugly purple tinge, but Emma Lou was certain that it made her skin look less dark.

She hailed a taxi and went to the Renaissance Casino. She did feel foolish, going there without an escort, but the doorman didn't seem to notice. Perhaps it was all right. Perhaps it was customary for Harlem girls to go about unaccompanied. She checked her wraps and wandered along the promenade that bordered the dance floor. It was early yet, just ten-thirty, and only a few couples were dancing. She found a chair, and tried to look as if she were waiting for some one. The orchestra stopped playing, people crowded past her. She liked the dance hall, liked its draped walls and ceilings, its harmonic color design and soft lights.

The music began again. She didn't see Jasper. A spindly legged yellow boy, awkward and bashful, asked her to dance with him. She did. The boy danced badly, but dancing with him was better than sitting there alone, looking foolish. She did wish that he would assume a more upright position and stop scrunching his shoulders. It seemed as if he were trying to bend both their backs to the breaking point. As they danced they talked about the music. He asked her did she have an escort. She said yes, and hurried to the ladies' room when the dance was over.

She didn't particularly like the looks of the crowd. It was well-behaved enough, but . . . well . . . one could see that they didn't belong to the cultured classes. They weren't the right sort of people. Maybe nice people didn't come here. Jasper hadn't been so nice. She wished she could see him, wouldn't she give him a piece of her mind?—And for the first time she really sensed the baseness of the trick he had played on her.

She walked out of the ladies' room and found herself again on the promenade. For a moment she stood there, watching the dancers. The floor was more crowded now, the dancers more numerous and gay. She watched them swirl and glide around the dance floor, and an intense longing for Jasper or John or any one welled up within her. It was terrible to be so alone, terrible to stand here and see other girls contentedly curled up in men's arms. She had been foolish to come; Jasper probably never came here. In truth he was no doubt far away from New York by now. What sense was there in her being here. She wasn't going to stay. She was going home, but before starting toward the check room, she took one more glance at the dancers and saw her cabaret dancing partner.

He was dancing with a slender brown-skin girl, his smile as ecstatic and intense as before. Emma Lou noted the pleasing lines of his body encased in a form-fitting blue suit. Why didn't he look her way?

"May I have this dance?" A well-modulated deep voice. A slender stripling, arrayed in brown, with a dark brown face. He had dimples. They danced. Emma Lou was having difficulty in keeping track of Alva. He seemed to be consciously striving to elude her. He seemed to be deliberately darting in among clusters of couples, where he would remain hidden for some time, only to reappear far ahead or behind her.

Her partner was congenial. He introduced himself, but she did not hear his name, for at that moment, Alva and his partner glided close by. Emma Lou actually shoved the supple, slender boy she was dancing with in Alva's direction. She mustn't lose him this time. She must speak. They veered close to one another. They almost collided. Alva looked into her face. She smiled and spoke. He acknowledged her salute, but stared at her, frankly perplexed, and there was no recognition in his face as he moved away, bending his head close to that of his partner, the better to hear something she was asking him.

The slender brown boy clung to Emma Lou's arm, treated her to a soda, and, at her request, piloted her around the promenade. She saw Alva sitting in a box in the balcony, and suggested to her companion that they parade around the balcony for a while. He assented. He was lonesome, too. First summer in New York. Just graduated from Virginia Union University. Going to Columbia School of Law next year. Nice boy, but no appeal. Too—supple.

They passed by Alva's box. He wasn't there. Two other couples and the girl he had been dancing with were. Emma Lou and her companion walked the length of the balcony, then retraced their steps just in time to see Alva coming around the corner carrying a cup of water. She watched the rhythmic swing of his legs, like symmetrical pendulums, perfectly shaped; and she admired once more the intriguing lines of his body and pleasing foreignness of his face. As they met, she smiled at him. He was certain he did not know her but he stopped and was polite, feeling that he must find out who she was and where he had met her.

"How do you do?" Emma Lou held out her hand. He shifted the cup of water from his right hand to his left. "I'm glad to see you again." They shook hands. His clasp was warm, his palm soft and sweaty. The supple lad stepped to one side. "I—I," Emma Lou was speaking now, "have often wondered if we would meet again." Alva wanted to laugh. He could not imagine who this girl with the purple-powdered skin was. Where had he seen her? She must be mistaking him for some one else. Well, he was game. He spoke sincerely:

"And I, too, have wanted to see you."

Emma Lou couldn't blush, but she almost blubbered with joy.

"Perhaps we'll have a dance together."

"My God," thought Alva, "she's a quick worker."

"Oh, certainly, where can I find you?"

"Downstairs on the promenade, near the center boxes."

"The one after this?" This seemed to be the easiest way out. He could easily dodge her later.

"Yes," and she moved away, the supple lad clinging to her arm again.

"Who's the 'spade,' Alva?" Geraldine had seen him stop to talk to her.

"Damned if I know."

"Aw, sure you know who she is. You danced with her at Small's." Braxton hadn't forgotten.

"Well, I never. Is that *it?*" Laughter all around as he told about their first meeting. But he didn't dodge her, for Geraldine and Braxton riled him with their pertinacious badinage. He felt that they were making more fun of him than of her, and to show them just how little he minded their kidding he stalked off to find her. She was waiting, the slim, brown stripling swaying beside her, importuning her not to wait longer. He didn't want to lose her. She didn't want to lose Alva, and was glad when they danced off together.

"Who's your boy friend?" Alva had fortified himself with gin. His breath smelled familiar.

"Just an acquaintance." She couldn't let him know that she had come here unescorted. "I didn't think you'd remember me."

"Of course, I did; how could I forget you?" Smooth tongue, phrases with a double meaning.

"I didn't forget *you*." Emma Lou was being coy. "I have often looked for you."

Looked for him where? My God, what an impression he must have made! He wondered what he had said to her before. Plunge in boy, plunge! The blacker the berry—he chuckled to himself.

Orchestra playing "Blue Skies," as an especial favor to her. Alva telling her his name and giving her his card, and asking her to 'phone him some day. Alva close to her and being nice, his arms tightening about her. She would call him tomorrow. Ecstasy ended too soon. The music stopped. He thanked her for the dance and left her standing on the promenade by the side of the waiting slender stripling. She danced with him twice more, then let him take her home.

At ten the next morning Emma Lou called Alva. Braxton came to the telephone.

"Alva's gone to work; who is it?" People should have more sense than to call that early in the morning. He never got up until noon. Emma Lou was being apologetic.

"Could you tell me what time he will be in?"

"'Bout six-thirty. Who shall I say called? This is his room-mate."

"Just . . . Oh . . . I'll call him later. Thank you."

Braxton swore. "Why in the hell does Alva give so many damn women his 'phone number?"

Six-thirty-five. His roommate had said about six-thirty. She called again. He came to the 'phone. She thought his voice was more harsh than usual.

"Oh, I'm all right, only tired."

"Did you work hard?"

"I always work hard."

"I . . . I . . . just thought I'd call."

"Glad you did, call me again some time. Good-bye"—said too quickly. No chance to say "When will I see you again?"

She went home, got into the bed, and cried herself to sleep.

Arline returned two days ahead of schedule. Things settled

back into routine. The brown stripling had taken Emma Lou out twice, but upon her refusal to submit herself to him, had gone away in a huff, and had not returned. She surmised that it was the first time he had made such a request of any one. He did it so ineptly. Work. Home. Walks. Theaters downtown during the afternoon, and thoughts of Alva. Finally, she just had to call him again. He came to the 'phone:

"Hello. Who? Emma Lou? Where have you been? I've been wondering where you were?"

She was shy, afraid she might be too bold. But Alva had had his usual three glasses of before-dinner gin. He helped her out.

"When can I see you, Sugar?"

Sugar! He had called her "sugar." She told him where she worked. He was to meet her after the theater that very night.

"How many nights a week you gonna have that little inkspitter up here?"

"Listen here, Brax, you have who you want up here, don't you?"

"That ain't it. I just don't like to see you tied up with a broad like that."

"Why not? She's just as good as the rest, and you know what they say, 'The blacker the berry, the sweeter the juice.'"

"The only thing a black woman is good for is to make money for a brown-skin papa."

"I guess I don't know that."

"Well," Braxton was satisfied now, "if that's the case . . ."

He had faith in Alva's wisdom.

Part 4

Rent Party

Saturday evening. Alva had urged her to hurry uptown from work. He was going to take her on a party with some friends of his. This was the first time he had ever asked her to go to any sort of social affair with him. She had never met any of his friends save Braxton, who scarcely spoke to her, and never before had Alva suggested taking her to any sort of social gathering either public or semi-public. He often took her to various motion picture theaters, both downtown and in Harlem, and at least three nights a week he would call for her at the theater and escort her to Harlem. On these occasions they often went to Chinese restaurants or to ice cream parlors before going home. But usually they would go to City College Park, find an empty bench in a dark corner where they could sit and spoon before retiring either to her room or to Alva's.

Emma Lou had, long before this, suggested going to a dance or to a party, but Alva had always countered that he never attended such affairs during the summer months, that he stayed away from them for precisely the same reason that he stayed away from work, namely, because it was too hot. Dancing, said he, was a matter of calisthenics, and calisthenics were work. Therefore it, like any sort of physical exercise, was taboo during hot weather.

Alva sensed that sooner or later Emma Lou would become aware of his real reason for not taking her out among his friends. He realized that one as color-conscious as she appeared to be would, at some not so distant date, jump to what for him would be uncomfortable conclusions. He did not wish to risk losing her before the end of summer, but neither could he risk taking her out among his friends, for he knew too well that he would be derided for his unseemly preference for "dark meat," and told publicly without regard for her feelings, that "black cats must go."

Furthermore he always took Geraldine to parties and dances. Geraldine with her olive-colored skin and straight black hair. Geraldine, who of all the people he pretended to love, really inspired him emotionally as well as physically, the one person he conquested without thought of monetary gain. Yet he had to do something with Emma Lou, and release from the quandary presented itself from most unexpected quarters.

Quite accidentally, as things of the sort happen in Harlem with its complex but interdependable social structure, he had become acquainted with a young Negro writer, who had asked him to escort a group of young writers and artists to a house-rent party. Though they had heard much of this phenomenon, none had been on the inside of one, and because of their rather polished manners and exteriors, were afraid that they might not be admitted. Proletarian Negroes are as suspicious of their more sophisticated brethren as they are of white men, and resent as keenly their intrusions into their social world. Alva had consented to act as cicerone, and, realizing that these people would be more or less free from the color prejudice exhibited by his other friends, had decided to take Emma Lou along, too. He was also aware of her intellectual pretensions, and felt that she would be especially pleased to meet recognized talents and outstanding personalities. She did not have to know that these were not his regular companions, and from then on she would have no reason to feel that he was ashamed to have her meet his friends.

Emma Lou could hardly attend to Arline's change of complexion and clothes between acts and scenes, so anxious was she to get to Alva's house and to the promised party. Her happiness was complete. She was certain now that Alva loved her, certain that he was not ashamed or even aware of her dusky complexion. She had felt from the first that he was superior to such inane truck, now she knew it. Alva loved her for herself alone, and loved her so much that he didn't mind her being a coal scuttle blond.

Sensing something unusual, Arline told Emma that she would remove her own makeup after the performance, and let her have time to get dressed for the party. This she proceeded to do all through the evening, spending much time in front of the mirror at Arline's dressing table, manicuring her nails, marcelling her hair, and applying various creams and cosmetics to her face in order to make her despised darkness less obvious. Finally, she put on one of Arline's less pretentious afternoon frocks, and set out for Alva's house.

As she approached his room door, she heard much talk and laughter, moving her to halt and speculate whether or not she should go in. Even her unusual and high-tensioned jubilance was not powerful enough to overcome immediately her shyness and fears. Suppose these friends of Alva's would not take kindly to her? Suppose they were like Braxton, who invariably curled his lip when he saw her, and seldom spoke even as much as a word of greeting? Suppose they were like the people who used to attend her mother's and grandmother's teas, club meetings, and receptions, dismissing her with—"It beats me how this child of yours looks so unlike the rest of you. . . . Are you sure it isn't adopted." Or suppose they were like the college youth she had known in Southern California? No, that couldn't be. Alva would never invite her where she would not be welcome. These were his friends. And so was Braxton, but Alva said he was peculiar. There was no danger. Alva had invited her. She was here. Anyway she wasn't so black. Hadn't she artificially lightened her skin about four or five shades until she was almost brown? Certainly it was all right. She needn't be a foolish ninny all her life. Thus, reassured, she knocked on the door, and felt herself trembling with excitement and internal uncertainty as Alva let her in, took her hat and coat, and proceeded to introduce her to the people in the room.

"Miss Morgan, meet Mr. Tony Crews. You've probably seen his book of poems. He's the little jazz boy, you know."

"Emma Lou bashfully touched the extended hand of the curly-headed poet. She had not seen or read his book, but she had often noticed his name in the newspapers and magazines. He was all that she had expected him to be except that he had pimples on his face. These didn't fit in with her mental picture.

"Miss Morgan, this is Cora Thurston. Maybe I should'a introduced you ladies first."

"I'm no lady, and I hope you're not either, Miss Morgan." She smiled, shook Emma Lou's hand, then turned away to continue her interrupted conversation with Tony Crews.

"Miss Morgan, meet . . . ," he paused, and addressed a tall, dark yellow youth stretched out on the floor, "What name you going by now?"

The boy looked up and smiled.

"Why, Paul, of course."

"All right then, Miss Morgan, this is Mr. Paul, he changes his name every season."

Emma Lou sought to observe this person more closely, and was shocked to see that his shirt was open at the neck and that he was sadly in need of a haircut and shave.

"Miss Morgan, meet Mr. Walter." A small slender dark youth with an infectious smile and small features. His face was familiar. Where had she seen him before?

"Now that you've met every one, sit down on the bed there beside Truman and have a drink. Go on with your talk folks," he urged as he went over to the dresser to fill a glass with a milk-colored liquid. Cora Thurston spoke up in answer to Alva's adjuration:

"Guess there ain't much more to say. Makes me mad to discuss it anyhow."

"No need of getting mad at people like that," said Tony Crews simply and softly. "I think one should laugh at such stupidity."

"And ridicule it, too," came from the luxurious person sprawled over the floor, for he did impress Emma Lou as being luxurious, despite the fact that his suit was unpressed, and that he wore neither socks nor necktie. She noticed the many graceful gestures he made with his hands, but wondered why he kept

twisting his lips to one side when he talked. Perhaps he was trying to mask the size of his mouth.

Truman was speaking now, "Ridicule will do no good, nor
mere laughing at them. I admit those weapons are about the
only ones an intelligent person would use, but one must also
admit that they are rather futile."

"Why futile?" Paul queried indolently.

"They are futile," Truman continued, "because, well, those
people cannot help being like they are——their environment has
made them that way."

Miss Thurston muttered something. It sounded like "hooey,"
then held out an empty glass. "Give me some more firewater,
Alva." Alva hastened across the room and re-filled her glass.
Emma Lou wondered what they were talking about. Again Cora
broke the silence, "You can't tell me they can't help it. They kick
about white people, then commit the same crime."

There was a knock on the door, interrupting something Tony
Crews was about to say. Alva went to the door.

"Hello, Ray." A tall, blond, fair-skinned youth entered. Emma
Lou gasped, and was more bewildered than ever. All of this silly
talk and drinking, and now—here was a white man!

"Hy, everybody, Jusas Chraust, I hope you saved me some
liquor." Tony Crews held out his empty glass and said quietly,
"We've had about umpteen already, so I doubt if there's any
more left."

You can't kid me, Bo. I know Alva would save me a dram or
two." Having taken off his hat and coat he squatted down on the
floor beside Paul.

Truman turned to Emma Lou. "Oh, Ray, meet Miss Morgan.
Mr. Jorgenson, Miss Morgan."

"Glad to know you; pardon my not getting up, won't you?"
Emma Lou didn't know what to say, and couldn't think of anything appropriate, but since he was smiling, she tried to smile,
too, and nodded her head.

"What's the big powwow?" he asked. "All of you look so serious. Haven't you had enough liquor, or are you just trying to
settle the ills of the universe?"

"Neither," said Paul. "They're just damning our 'pink niggers.'"

Emma Lou was aghast. Such extraordinary people—saying "nigger" in front of a white man! Didn't they have any race pride or proper bringing up? Didn't they have any common sense?

"What've they done now?" Ray asked, reaching out to accept the glass Alva was handing him.

"No more than they've always done," Tony Crews answered. "Cora here just felt like being indignant, because she heard of a forthcoming wedding in Brooklyn to which the prospective bride and groom have announced they will not invite any dark people."

"Seriously now," Truman began. Ray interrupted him.

"Who in the hell wants to be serious?"

"As I was saying," Truman continued, "you can't blame light Negroes for being prejudiced against dark ones. All of you know that white is the symbol of everything pure and good, whether that everything be concrete or abstract. Ivory Soap is advertised as being ninety-nine and some fraction per cent pure, and Ivory Soap is white. Moreover, virtue and virginity are always represented as being clothed in white garments. Then, too, the God we, or rather most Negroes worship is a patriarchal white man, seated on a white throne, in a spotless white Heaven, radiant with white streets and white-apparelled angels eating white honey and drinking white milk."

"Listen to the boy rave. Give him another drink," Ray shouted, but Truman ignored him and went on, becoming more and more animated.

"We are all living in a totally white world, where all standards are the standards of the white man, and where almost invariably what the white man does is right, and what the black man does is wrong, unless it is precedented by something a white man has done.

"Which," Cora added scornfully, "makes it all right for light Negroes to discriminate against dark ones?"

"Not at all," Truman objected. "It merely explains, not justifies, the evil—or rather, the fact of intra-racial segregation. Mulattoes have always been accorded more consideration by white people than their darker brethren. They were made to

feel superior even during slave days . . . made to feel proud, as
Bud Fischer would say, that they were bastards. It was for the
mulatto offspring of white masters and Negro slaves that the
first schools for Negroes were organized, and say what you will,
it is generally the Negro with a quantity of mixed blood in his
veins who finds adaptation to a Nordic environment more easy
than one of pure blood, which, of course, you will admit, is, to
an American Negro, convenient if not virtuous."

"Does that justify their snobbishness and self-evaluated superiority?"

"No, Cora, it doesn't," returned Truman. "I'm not trying to
excuse them. I'm merely trying to give what I believe to be an
explanation of this thing. I have never been to Washington and
only know what Paul and you have told me about conditions
there, but they seem to be just about the same as conditions in
Los Angeles, Omaha, Chicago, and other cities in which I have
lived or visited. You see, people have to feel superior to something, and there is scant satisfaction in feeling superior to
domestic animals or steel machines that one can train or utilize.
It is much more pleasing to pick out some individual or some
group of individuals on the same plane to feel superior to. This
is almost necessary when one is a member of a supposedly
despised, mistreated minority group. Then consider that the
mulatto is much nearer white than he is black and is therefore
more liable to act like a white man than like a black one,
although I cannot say that I see a great deal of difference in any
of their actions. They are human beings first and only white or
black incidentally."

Ray pursed his lips and whistled.

"But you seem to forget," Tony Crews insisted, "that because
a man is dark, it doesn't necessarily mean he is not of mixed
blood. Now look at . . ."

"Yeah, let him look at you or at himself or at Cora," Paul interrupted. "There ain't no unmixed Negroes."

"But I haven't forgotten that," Truman said, ignoring the note
of finality in Paul's voice. "I merely took it for granted that we
were talking only about those Negroes who were light-
skinned."

"But all light-skinned Negroes aren't color struck or color prejudiced," interjected Alva, who, up to this time, like Emma Lou, had remained silent. This was, he thought, a strategic moment for him to say something, He hoped Emma Lou would get the full significance of this statement.

"True enough," Truman began again. "But I also took it for granted that we were only talking about those who were. As I said before, Negroes are, after all, human beings, and they are subject to be influenced and controlled by the same forces and factors that influence and control other human beings. In an environment where there are so many color-prejudiced whites, there are bound to be a number of color-prejudiced blacks. Color prejudice and religion are akin in one respect. Some folks have it and some don't, and the kernel that is responsible for it is present in us all, which is to say, that potentially we are all color-prejudiced as long as we remain in this environment. For, as you know, prejudices are always caused by differences, and the majority group sets the standard. Then, too, since black is the favorite color of vaudeville comedians and jokesters, and conversely, as intimately associated with tragedy, it is no wonder that even the blackest individual will seek out some one more black than himself to laugh at.

"So saith the Lord," Tony answered soberly.

"And the Holy Ghost saith, let's have another drink."

"Happy thought, Ray," returned Cora. "Give us some more ice cream and gin, Alva."

Alva went into the alcove to prepare another concoction. Tony started the victrola. Truman turned to Emma Lou, who, all this while, had been sitting there with Alva's arm around her, every muscle in her body feeling as if it wanted to twitch, not knowing whether to be sad or to be angry. She couldn't comprehend all of this talk. She couldn't see how these people could sit down and so dispassionately discuss something that seemed particularly tragic to her. This fellow Truman, whom she was certain she knew, with all his hi-faluting talk disgusted her immeasurably. She wasn't sure that they weren't all poking fun at her. Truman was speaking:

"Miss Morgan, didn't you attend school in Southern

California?" Emma Lou at last realized where she had seen him before. So *this* was Truman Walter, the little "cock o' the walk," as they had called him on the campus. She answered him with difficulty, for there was a sob in her throat. "Yes, I did." Before Truman could say more, Ray called to him:

"Say, Bozo, what time are we going to the party? It's almost one o'clock now."

"Is it?" Alva seemed surprised. "But Aaron and Alta aren't here yet."

"They've been married just long enough to be late to everything."

"What do you say we go by and ring their bell?" Tony suggested, ignoring Paul's Greenwich Village wit."

"'Sall right with me." Truman lifted his glass to his lips. "Then on to the house-rent party . . . on to the bawdy bowels of Beale Street!"

They drained their glasses and prepared to leave.

"Ahhhh, sock it." . . . "Ummmm" . . . Piano playing—slow, loud, and discordant, accompanied by the rhythmic sound of shuffling feet. Down a long, dark hallway, to an inside room, lit by a solitary red bulb. "Oh, play it you dirty no-gooder." . . . A room full of dancing couples, scarcely moving their feet, arms completely encircling one another's bodies . . . cheeks being warmed by one another's breath . . . eyes closed . . . animal ecstasy agitating their perspiring faces. There was much panting, much hip movement, much shaking of the buttocks. . . . "Do it twice in the same place." . . . "Git off that dime." Now somebody was singing, "I ask you very confidentially. . . ." "Sing it man, sing it." . . . Piano treble moaning, bass rumbling like thunder. A swarm of people, motivating their bodies to express in suggestive movements the ultimate consummation of desire.

The music stopped, the room was suffocatingly hot, and Emma Lou was disturbingly dizzy. She clung fast to Alva, and let the room and its occupants whirl around her. Bodies and faces glided by. Leering faces and lewd bodies. Anxious faces and angular bodies. Sad faces and obese bodies. All mixed up together. She began to wonder how such a small room could hold so many people. "Oh, play it again . . ." She saw the pianist now, silhouetted against the dark mahogany piano, saw him bend his long, slick-haired head, until it hung low on his chest, then lift his hands high in the air, and as quickly let them descend upon the keyboard. There was one moment of cacophony, then the long, supple fingers evolved a slow, tantalizing melody out of the deafening chaos.

Every one began to dance again. Body called to body, and cemented themselves together, limbs lewdly intertwined. A couple there kissing, another couple dipping to the floor, and slowly shimmying, belly to belly, as they came back to an upright position. A slender dark girl with wild eyes and wilder hair stood in the center of the room, supported by the strong, lithe arms of a longshoreman. She bent her trunk backward, until her head hung below her waistline, and all the while she kept the lower portion of her body quivering like jello.

"She whips it to a jelly," the piano player was singing now, and banging on the keys with such might that an empty gin bottle on top of the piano seemed to be seized with the ague. "Oh, play it Mr. Charlie." Emma Lou grew limp in Alva's arms.

"What's the matter, honey, drunk?" She couldn't answer. The music augmented by the general atmosphere of the room and the liquor she had drunk had presumably created another person in her stead. She felt like flying into an emotional frenzy—felt like flinging her arms and legs in insane unison. She had become very fluid, very elastic, and all the while she was giving in more and more to the music and to the liquor and to the physical madness of the moment.

When the music finally stopped, Alva led Emma Lou to a settee by the window which his crowd had appropriated. Every one was exceedingly animated, but they all talked in hushed, almost reverential tones.

"Isn't this marvelous?" Truman's eyes were ablaze with interest and excitement. Even Tony Crews seemed unusually alert.

"It's the greatest I've seen yet," he exclaimed.

Alva seemed the most unemotional one in the crowd. Paul the most detached. "Look at 'em all watching Ray."

"Remember, Bo," Truman counseled him. "Tonight you're 'passing.' Here's a new wrinkle, white man 'passes' for Negro."

"Why not?" Enough of you pass for white." They all laughed, then transferred their interest back to the party. Cora was speaking:

"Didya see that little girl in pink—the one with the scar on her face—dancing with that tall, lanky, one-armed man? Wasn't she throwing it up to him?"

"Yeah," Tony admitted, "but she didn't have anything on that little Mexican-looking girl. She musta been born in Cairo."

"Saay, but isn't that one bad-looking darkey over there, two chairs to the left; is he gonna smother that woman?" Truman asked excitedly.

"I'd say she kinda liked it," Paul answered, then lit another cigarette.

"Do you know they have corn liquor in the kitchen? They serve it from a coffee pot." Aaron seemed proud of his discovery.

"Yes," said Alva, "and they got hoppin'-john out there, too.

"What the hell is hoppin'-john?"

"Ray, I'm ashamed of you. Here you are passing for colored and don't know what hoppin'-john is!"

"Tell him, Cora, I don't know either."

"Another one of these foreigners." Cora looked at Truman disdainfully. "Hoppin'-john is blackeyed peas and rice. Didn't they have any out in Salt Lake City?"

"Have they any chitterlings?" Alta asked eagerly.

"No, Alta," Alva replied, dryly. "This isn't Kansas. They have got pig's feet though."

"Lead me to 'em," Aaron and Alta shouted in unison, and led the way to the kitchen. Emma Lou clung to Alva's arm and tried to remain behind. "Alva, I'm afraid."

"Afraid of what? Come on, snap out of it! You need another drink." He pulled her up from the settee and led her through the crowded room down the long dark hallway to the more crowded kitchen.

When they returned to the room, the pianist was just preparing to play again. He was tall and slender, with extra long legs and arms, giving him the appearance of a scarecrow. His pants

were tight in the waist and full in the legs. He wore no coat, and
a blue silk shirt hung damply to his body. He acted as if he were
king of the occasion, ruling all from his piano stool throne. He
talked familiarly to every one in the room, called women from
other men's arms, demanded drinks from any bottle he happened to see being passed around, laughed uproariously, and
made many grotesque and ofttimes obscene gestures.

There were sounds of a scuffle in an adjoining room, and an
excited voice exclaimed, "You goddam son-of-a-bitch, don't you
catch my dice no more." The paino player banged on the keys
and drowned out the reply, if there was one.

Emma Lou could not keep her eyes off the piano player. He
was acting like a maniac, occasionally turning completely around
on his stool, grimacing like a witch doctor, and letting his hands
dawdle over the keyboard of the piano with an agonizing indo-
lence, when compared to the extreme exertion to which he put
the rest of his body. He was improvising. The melody of the
piece he had started to play was merely a base for more bawdy
variations. His left foot thumped on the floor in time with the
music, while his right punished the piano's loud-pedal. Beads of
perspiration gathered grease from his slicked-down hair, and
rolled oleaginously down his face and neck, spotting the already
damp baby-blue shirt, and streaking his already greasy black
face with more shiny lanes.

A sailor lad suddenly ceased his impassioned hip movement
and strode out of the room, pulling his partner behind him,
pushing people out of the way as he went. The spontaneous
moans and slangy ejaculations of the piano player and of the
more articulate dancers became more regular, more like a
chanted obligato to the music. This lasted for a couple of hours
interrupted only by hectic intermissions. Then the dancers grew
less violent in their movements, and though the piano player
seemed never to tire there were fewer couples on the floor, and
those left seemed less loath to move their legs.

Eventually, the music stopped for a long interval, and there
was a more concerted drive on the kitchen's corn liquor supply.
Most of the private flasks and bottles were empty. There were
more calls for food, too, and the crap game in the side room

annexed more players and more kibitzers. Various men and women had disappeared altogether. Those who remained seemed worn and tired. There was much petty person-to-person badinage and many whispered consultations in corners. There was an argument in the hallway between the landlord and two couples, who wished to share one room without paying him more than the regulation three dollars required of one couple. Finally, Alva suggested they leave. Emma Lou had drifted off into a state of semi-consciousness and was too near asleep or drunk to distinguish people or voices. All she knew was that she was being led out of that dreadful place, that the perturbing "pilgrimage to the proletariat's parlor social," as Truman had called it, was ended, and that she was in a taxicab, cuddled up in Alva's arms.

Emma Lou awoke with a headache. Some one was knocking at her door, but when she first awakened it had seemed as if the knocking was inside of her head. She pressed her fingers to her throbbing temples and tried to become more conscious. The knock persisted and she finally realized that it was at her door rather than in her head. She called out, "Who is it?"

"It's me." Emma Lou was not far enough out of the fog to recognize who "me" was. It didn't seem important anyway, so without any more thought or action, she allowed herself to doze off again. Whoever was on the outside of the door banged the louder, and finally Emma Lou distinguished the voice of her landlady, calling, "Let me in, Miss Morgan, let me in." The voice grew more sharp . . . "Let me in," and in an undertone, "Must have some one in there." This last served to awaken Emma Lou more fully, and though every muscle in her body protested, she finally got out of bed and went to the door. The lady entered precipitously, and pushing Emma Lou aside sniffed the air and looked around as if she expected to surprise some one, either squeezing under the bed or leaping through the window. After she had satisfied herself that there was no one else in the room, she turned to Emma Lou furiously:

"Miss Morgan, I wish to talk to you." Emma Lou closed the door and wearily sat down upon the bed. The wrinkle-faced old woman glared at her and shifted the position of her snuff so she could talk more easily. "I won't have it, I tell you, I won't have it." Emma Lou tried hard to realize what it was she wouldn't have, and failing, she said nothing, just screwed up her eyes and tried to look sober.

"Do you hear me?" Emma Lou nodded. "I won't have it. When you moved in here I thought I made it clear that I was a respectable woman and that I kept a respectable house. Do you understand now?" Emma Lou nodded again. There didn't seem to be anything else to do. "I'm glad you do. Then it won't be necessary for me to explain why I want my room."

Emma Lou unscrewed her eyes and opened her mouth. What was this woman talking about? "I don't think I understand."

The old lady was quick with her answer. "There ain't nothin' for you to understand, but that I want you to get out of my house. I don't have no such carryings-on around here. A drunken woman in my house at all hours in the morning, being carried in by a man! Well, you coulda knocked me over with a feather."

At last Emma Lou began to understand. Evidently the land-lady had seen her when she had come in, no doubt had seen Alva carry her to her room, and perhaps had listened outside the door. She was talking again:

"You must get out. Your week is up Wednesday. That gives you three days to find another room, and I want you to act like a lady the rest of that time, too. The idea!" she sputtered, and stalked out of the room.

This is a pretty mess, thought Emma Lou. Yet she found her-self unable to think or do anything about it. Her lethargic state worried her. Here she was about to be dispossessed by an irate landlady, and all she could do about it was sit on the side of her bed and think—maybe I ought to take a dose of salts. Momentarily, she had forgotten it was Sunday, and began to wonder how near time it was for her to go to work. She was surprised to discover that it was still early in the forenoon. She couldn't possibly have gone to bed before four-thirty or five, yet it seemed as if she had slept for hours. She felt like some one who had been under the influence of some sinister potion for a long period of time. Had she been drugged? Her head still throbbed, her insides burned, her tongue was swollen, her lips chapped and feverish. She began to deplore her physical condition, and even to berate herself and Alva for last night's debauchery.

Funny people, his friends. Come to think of it, they were all very much different from any one else she had ever known. They were all so, so—she sought for a descriptive word, but could think of nothing save that revolting, "Oh, sock it," she had heard on first entering the apartment where the house-rent party had been held.

Then she began to wonder about her landlady's charges. There was no need arguing about the matter. She had wanted to move anyway. Maybe now she could go ahead and find a decent place in which to live. She had never had the nerve to begin another room-hunting expedition after the last one. She shuddered as she thought about it, then climbed back into the bed. She could see no need in staying up so long as her head ached as it did. She wondered if Alva had made much noise in bringing her in, wondered how long he had stayed, and if he had had any trouble manipulating the double-barreled police lock on the outside door. Harlem people were so careful about barricading themselves in. They all seemed to fortify themselves, not only against strangers, but against neighbors and friends as well.

And Alva? She had to admit she was a trifle disappointed in him and his friends. They certainly weren't what she would have called either intellectuals or respectable people. Whoever heard of decent folk attending such a lascivious festival? She remembered their enthusiastic comments and tried to comprehend just what it was that had intrigued and interested them. Looking for material, they had said. More than likely they were looking for liquor and a chance to be licentious.

Alva himself worried her a bit. She couldn't understand why gin seemed so indispensable to him. He always insisted that he had to have at least three drinks a day. Once she had urged him not to follow this program. Unprotestingly, he had come to her the following evening without the usual juniper berry smell on his breath, but he had been so disagreeable and had seemed so

much like a worn out and dissipated person that she had never
again suggested that he not have his usual quota of drinks. Then,
too, she had discovered that he was much too lovable after having had his "evening drams" to be discouraged from taking
them. Emma Lou had never met any one in her life who was as
loving and kind to her as Alva. He seemed to anticipate her
every mood and desire, and he was the most soothing and satisfying person with whom she had ever come into contact. He
seldom riled her—seldom ruffled her feelings. He seemed to
give in to her on every occasion, and was the most chivalrous
escort imaginable. He was always courteous, polite, and thought-
ful of her comfort.

As yet she had been unable to become angry with him. Alva
never argued or protested unduly. Although Emma Lou didn't
realize it, he used more subtle methods. His means of remaining
master of all situations were both tactful and sophisticated; for
example, Emma Lou never realized just how she had first begun
giving him money. Surely he hadn't asked her for it. It had just
seemed the natural thing to do after a while, and she had done
it, willingly and without question. The ethical side of their relationship never worried her. She was content and she was happy—at least she was in possession of something that seemed to
bring her happiness. She seldom worried about Alva not being
true to her, and if she questioned him about such matters, he
would pretend not to hear her and change the conversation. The
only visible physical reaction would be a slight narrowing of the
eyes, as if he were trying not to wince from the pain of some
inner hurt.

Once she had suggested marriage, and had been shocked
when Alva told her that to him the marriage ceremony seemed
a waste of time. He had already been married twice, and he
hadn't even bothered to obtain a divorce from his first wife
before acquiring number two. On hearing this, Emma Lou had
urged him to tell her more about these marital experiments, and
after a little coaxing, he had done so, very impassively and very
sketchily, as if he were relating the experiences of another. He
told her that he had really loved his first wife, but that she was
such an essential polygamous female that he had been forced to

abdicate and hand her over to the multitudes. According to
Alva, she had been as vain as Braxton, and as fundamentally
dependent upon flattery. She could go without three square
meals a day, but she couldn't do without her contingent of
mealy-mouthed admirers, all eager to outdo one another in the
matter of compliments. One man could never have satisfied her,
not that she was a nymphomaniac with abnormal physical appe-
tites, but because she wanted attention, and the more men she
had around her, the more attention she could receive. She
hadn't been able to convince Alva, though, that her battalion of
admirers were all of the platonic variety. "I know niggers too
well," Alva had summed it up to Emma Lou, "so I told her she
just must go, and she went."

"But," Emma Lou had queried when he had started to talk
about something else, "what about your second wife?"

"Oh," he laughed, "well I married her when I was drunk. She
was an old woman about fifty. She kept me drunk from Sunday
to Sunday. When I finally got sober she showed me the marriage license and I well nigh passed out again."

"But where is she?" Emma Lou had asked, "and how did they
let you get married while you were drunk and already had a
wife?"

Alva shrugged his shoulders. "I don't know where she is. I
ain't seen her since I left her room that day. I sent Braxton up
there to talk to her. Seems like she'd been drunk, too. So, it
really didn't matter. And as for a divorce, I know plenty spades
right here in Harlem get married any time they want to. Who in
hell's gonna take the trouble getting a divorce when, if you
marry and already have a wife, you can get another without
going through all that red tape?"

Emma Lou had had to admit that this sounded logical, if ille-
gal. Yet she hadn't been convinced. "But," she insisted, "don't
they look you up and convict you of bigamy?"

"Hell, no. The only thing the law bothers niggers about is for
stealing, murdering, or chasing white women, and as long as
they don't steal from or murder ofays, the law ain't none too
particular about bothering them. The only time they act about
bigamy is when one of the wives squawk, and they hardly ever

do that. They're only too glad to see the old man get married again—then they can do likewise, without spending lots of time on lawyers and courthouse red tape."

This, and other things which Emma Lou had elicited from Alva, had convinced her that he was undoubtedly the most interesting person she had ever met. What added to this was the strange fact that he seemed somewhat cultured despite his admitted unorganized and haphazard early training. On being questioned, he advanced the theory that perhaps this was due to his long period of service as waiter and valet to socially prominent white people. Many Negroes, he had explained, even of the "dicty" variety, had obtained their *savoir faire* and knowledge of the social niceties in this manner.

Emma Lou lay abed, remembering the many different conversations they had had together, most of which had taken place on a bench in City College Park, or in Alva's room. With enough gin for stimulation, Alva could tell many tales of his life and hold her spellbound with vivid descriptions of the various situations he had found himself in. He loved to reminisce, when he found a good listener, and Emma Lou loved to listen when she found a good talker. Alva often said that he wished some one would write a story of his life. Maybe that was why he cultivated an acquaintance with these writer people. . . . Then it seemed as if this one-sided conversational communion strengthened their physical bond. It made Emma Lou more palatable to Alva, and it made Alva a more glamorous figure to Emma Lou.

But here she was day dreaming when she should be wondering where she was going to move. She couldn't possibly remain in this place, even if the old lady relented and decided to give her another chance to be respectable. Somehow or other she felt she had been insulted and, for the first time, began to feel angry with the old snuff-chewing termagant.

Her head ached no longer, but her body was still lethargic. Alva, Alva, Alva. Could she think of nothing else? Supposing she sat upright in the bed—supposing she and Alva were to live together. They might get a small apartment and be with one another entirely. Immediately she was all activity. The headache was forgotten. Out of bed, into her bathrobe, and down the hall to the bathroom. Even the quick shower seemed to be a slow, tedious process, and she was in such a hurry to hasten into the street and telephone Alva, in order to tell him of her new plans, that she almost forgot to make the very necessary and very customary application of bleaching cream to her face. As it was, she forgot to rinse her face and hands in lemon juice.

Alva had lost all patience with Braxton, and profanely told him so. No matter what his condition, Braxton would not work. He seemed to believe that because he was handsome, and because he was Braxton, he shouldn't have to work. He graced the world with his presence. Therefore, it should pay him. "A thing of beauty is a joy forever," and should be sustained by a communal larder. Alva tried to show him that such a larder didn't exist, that one either worked or hustled.

But as Alva had explained to Emma Lou, Braxton wouldn't work, and as a hustler he was a distinct failure. He couldn't gamble successfully, he never had a chance to steal, and he always allowed his egotism to defeat his own ends when he tried to get money from women. He assumed that at a word from him, anybody's pocketbook should be at his disposal, and that his handsomeness and personality were a combination none could withstand. It is a platitude among sundry sects and individuals that as a person thinketh, so he is, but it was not within the power of Braxton's mortal body to become the being his imagination sought to create. He insisted, for instance, that he was a golden brown replica of Rudolph Valentino. Every picture he could find of the late lamented cinema sheik he pasted either on the wall or on some of his belongings. The only reason that likenesses of his idol did not decorate all the wall space was because Alva objected to this flapperish ritual. Braton emulated his silver screen mentor in every way, watched his every gesture on the screen, then would stand in front of his mirror at home and practice Rudy's poses and facial expressions. Strange as it may seem, there was a certain likeness between the two, especially at such moments when Braxton would suddenly stand in the center of the floor and give a spontaneous impersonation of Rudy making love or conquering enemies. Then, at all times,

Braxton held his head as Rudy held his, and had even learned
how to smile and how to use his eyes in the same captivating
manner. But his charms were too obviously cultivated, and his
technique too clumsy. He would attract almost any one to him,
but they were sure to bolt away as suddenly as they had come.
He could have, but he could not hold.

Now, as Alva told Emma Lou, this was a distinct handicap to
one who wished to be a hustler, and live by one's wits off the
bounty of others. And the competition was too keen in a place
like Harlem, where the adaptability to city ways sometimes took
strange and devious turns, for a bungler to have much success.
Alva realized this, if Braxton didn't, and tried to tell him so, but
Braxton wouldn't listen. He felt that Alva was merely being
envious——the fact that Alva had more suits than he, and that
Alva always had clean shirts, liquor money and room rent, and
that Alva could continue to have these things, despite the fact
that he had decided to quit work during the hot weather, meant
nothing to Braxton at all. He had facial and physical perfection,
a magnetic body and much sex appeal. Ergo, he was a master.

However, lean days were upon him. His mother and aunt had
unexpectedly come to New York to help him celebrate the closing day of his freshman year at Columbia. His surprise at seeing
them was nothing in comparison to their surprise in finding that
their darling had not even started his freshman year. The aunt
was stoic——"What could you expect of a child with all that wild
Indian blood in him? Now, our people . . ." She hadn't liked
Braxton's father. His mother simply could not comprehend his
duplicity. Such an unnecessarily cruel and deceptive performance was beyond her understanding. Had she been told that
he was guilty of thievery, murder, or rape, she could have borne
up and smiled through her tears in true maternal fashion, but
that he could so completely fool her for nine months—incredi-
ble; preposterous, it just couldn't be!

She and her sister returned to Boston, telling every one there
what a successful year their darling had had at Columbia, and
telling Braxton before they left that he could not have another
cent of their money that summer, that if he didn't enter
Columbia in the fall . . . well, he was not yet of age. They made

many vague threats; none so alarming, however, as the threat of
a temporary, if not permanent, suspension of his allowance.

By pawning some of his suits, his watch, and diamond ring, he
amassed a small stake and took to gambling. Unlucky at love, he
should, so Alva said, have been lucky at cards, and was. But even
a lucky man will suffer from lack of skill and foolhardiness.
Braxton would gamble only with mature men who gathered in
the police-protected clubs, rather than with young chaps like
himself, who gathered in private places. He couldn't classify
himself with the cheap or the lowly. If he was to gamble, he
must gamble in a professional manner, with professional men.
As in all other affairs, he had luck, but no skill and little sense.
His little gambling stake lasted but a moment, flitted from him
feverishly, and left him holding an empty purse.

Then he took to playing the "numbers," placing quarters and
half dollars on a number compounded of three digits and anxiously perusing the daily clearing house reports to see whether
or not he had chosen correctly. Alva, too, played the numbers
consistently and, somehow or other, managed to remain ahead
of the game, but Braxton, as was to be expected, "hit" two or
three times, then grew excited over his winnings and began to
play two or three or even five dollars daily on one number. Such
plunging, unattended by scientific observation or close calcula-
tion, put him so far behind the game that his winnings were
soon dissipated and he had to stop playing altogether.

Alva had quit work for the summer. He contended that it was
far too hot to stand over a steam pressing machine during the
sultry summer months, and there was no other congenial work
available. Being a bellhop in one of the few New York hotels
where colored boys were used called for too long hours and
broken shifts. Then they didn't pay much money and he hated
to work for tips. He certainly would not take an elevator job,
paying only sixty or sixty-five dollars a month at most, and making it necessary for him to work nights one week from six to
eight, and days the next week, vice versa. Being an elevator
operator in a loft building required too much skill, patience and
muscular activity. The same could be said of the shipping clerk
positions, open in the various wholesale houses. He couldn't, of

course, be expected to be a porter, and swing a mop. Boot-blacking was not even to be considered. There was nothing left. He was unskilled, save as a presser. Once he had been appren-ticed to a journeyman tailor, but he preferred to forget that.

No, there was nothing he could do, and there was no sense in working in the summer. He never had done it; at least, not since he had been living in New York—so he didn't see why he should do it now. Furthermore, his salary hardly paid his saloon bill, and since his board and room and laundry and clothes came from other sources, why not quit work altogether and develop these sources to their capacity output? Things looked much brighter this year than ever before. He had more clothes, he had "hit" the numbers more than ever, he had won a baseball pool of no mean value, and, in addition to Emma Lou, he had made many other profitable contacts during the spring and winter months. It was safe for him to loaf, but he couldn't carry Braxton, or rather, he wouldn't. Yet he liked him well enough not to kick him into the streets. Something, he told Emma Lou, should be done for him first, so Alva started doing things.

First, he got him a girl, or rather steered him in the direction of one who seemed to be a good bet. She was. And as usual, Braxton had little trouble in attracting her to him. She was a simple-minded over-sexed little thing from a small town in Central Virginia, new to Harlem, and had hitherto always lived in her home town where she had been employed since her twelfth year as a maid-of-all-work to a wealthy white family. For four years, she had been her master's concubine, and probably would have continued in that capacity for an unspecified length of time had not the mistress of the house decided that after all it might not be good for her two adolescent sons to become aware of their father's philandering. She had had to accept it. Most of the women of her generation and in her circle had done likewise. But these were post-world war days of modernity . . . and, well, it just wasn't being done, what with the growing intel-ligence of the "darkies," and the increased sophistication of the children.

So Anise Hamilton had been surreptitiously shipped away to New York, and a new maid-of-all-work had mysteriously appeared in her place. The mistress had seen to it that this new maid was not as desirable as Anise, but a habit is a habit, and the master of the house was not the sort to substitute one habit for another. If anything, his wife had made herself more miserable by the change, since the last girl loved much better than she worked, while Anise proved competent on both scores, thereby pleasing both master and mistress.

Anise had come to Harlem and deposited the money her former mistress had supplied her with in the postal savings. She wouldn't hear to placing it in any other depository. Banks had a curious and discomforting habit of closing their doors without warning, and without the foresight to provide their patrons with another nest egg. If banks in Virginia went broke, those in wicked New York would surely do so. Now, Uncle Sam had the whole country behind him, and everybody knew that the United States was the most wealthy of the world's nations. Therefore, what safer place than the post office for one's bank account?

Anise got a job, too, almost immediately. Her former mistress had given her a letter to a friend of hers on Park Avenue, and this friend had another friend who had a sister who wanted a stock girl in her exclusive modiste shop. Anise was the type to grace such an establishment as this person owned, just the right size to create a smart uniform for, and shapely enough to allow the creator of the uniform ample latitude for bizarre experimentation.

Most important of all, her skin, the color of beaten brass with copper overtones, synchronized with the gray plaster walls, dark hardwood furniture and powder blue rugs in the Maison Quantrelle.

Anise soon had any number of "boy friends," with whom she had varying relations. But she willingly dropped them all for Braxton, and, simple village girl that she was, expected him to do likewise with his "girl friends." She had heard much about the "two-timing sugar daddies" in Harlem, and while she was well versed in the art herself, having never been particularly true to her male employer, she did think that this sort of thing was different, and that any time she was willing to play fair, her consort should do likewise.

Alva was proud of himself when he noticed how rapidly things progressed between Anise and Braxton. They were together constantly, and Anise, not unused to giving her home town "boy friends" some of "Mister Bossman's bounty," was soon slipping Braxton spare change to live on. Then she undertook to pay his half of the room rent, and finally, within three weeks, was, as Alva phrased it, "treating Braxton royally."

But as ever, he was insistent upon being perverse. His old swank and swagger was much in evidence. With most of his clothing out of the pawnshop, he attempted to dazzle the Avenue when he paraded its length, the alluring Anise, attired in clothes borrowed from her employer's stockroom, beside him. The bronze replica of Rudolph Valentino was, in the argot of Harlem's pool hall Johnnies, "out the barrel." The world was his. He had it in a bottle, and he need only make it secure by corking. But Braxton was never the person to make anything secure. He might manage to capture the entire universe, but he could never keep it pent up, for he would soon let it alone to look for two more like it. It was to be expected, then, that Braxton would lose his head. He did, deliberately and diabolically. Because Anise was so madly in love with him, he imagined that all other women should do as she had done, and how much more delightful and profitable it would be to have two or three Anises instead of one. So he began a crusade, spending much of Anise's money for campaign funds. Alva quarreled, and Anise threatened, but Braxton continued to explore and to expend.

Anise finally revolted when Braxton took another girl to a dance on her money. He had done this many times before, but she hadn't known about it. She wouldn't have known about it this time if he hadn't told her. He often did things like that. Thought it made him more desirable. Despite her simple-mindedness, Anise had spunk. She didn't like to quarrel, but she wasn't going to let any one make a fool out of her, so, the next week after the heartbreaking incident, she had moved and left no forwarding address. It was presumed that she had gone downtown to live in the apartment of the woman for whom she worked. Braxton seemed unconcerned about her disappearance, and continued his peacock-like march for some time, with feathers unruffled, even by frequent trips to the pawnshop. But a peacock can hardly preen an unplumaged body, and, though Braxton continued to strut, in a few weeks after the break, he was only a sad semblance of his former self.

Alva nagged at him continually. "Damned if I'm going to carry you." Braxton would remain silent. "You're the most no-count nigger I know. If you can't do anything else, why in the hell don't you get a job?" "I don't see you working," Braxton would answer.

"And you don't see me starving, either," would be the comeback.

"Oh, jost 'cause you got that little black wench . . ."

"That's all right about the little black wench. She's forty with me, and I know how to treat her. I bet you couldn't get five cents out of her."

"I wouldn't try."

"Hell, if you tried it wouldn't make no difference. There's a gal ready to pay to have a man, and there are lots more like her. You couldn't even keep a good-looking gold mine like Anise. Wish I could find her."

Braxton would sulk a while, thinking that his silence would discourage Alva, but Alva was not to be shut up. He was truly outraged. He felt that he was being imposed upon, being used by some one who thought himself superior to him. He would admit that he wasn't as handsome as Braxton, but he certainly had more common sense. The next Monday Braxton moved.

Alva was to take Emma Lou to the midnight show at the Lafayette Theater. He met her as she left work and they had taken the subway uptown. On the train they began to talk, shouting into one another's ears, trying to make their voices heard above the roar of the underground tube.

"Do you like your new home?" Alva shouted. He hadn't seen her since she had moved two days before.

"It's nice," she admitted loudly, "but it would be nicer if I had you there with me."

He patted her hand and held it regardless of the onlooking crowd.

"Maybe so, Sugar, but you wouldn't like me if you had to live with me all the time."

Emma Lou was aggrieved: "I don't see how you can say that. How do you know? That's what made me mad last Sunday."

Alva saw that Emma Lou was ready for an argument and he had no intention of favoring her, or of discomfiting himself. He was even sorry that he said as much as he had when she had first broached the "living together" matter over the telephone on Sunday, calling him out of bed before noon while Geraldine was there, too, looking, but not asking, for information. He smiled at her indulgently:

"If you say another word about it, I'll kiss you right here in the subway."

Emma Lou didn't put it beyond him so she could do nothing but smile and shut up. She rather liked him to talk to her that way. Alva was shouting into her ear again, telling her a scandalous tale he claimed to have heard while playing poker with some of the boys. He thus contrived to keep her entertained until they reached the 135th Street station where they finally emerged from beneath the pavement to mingle with the frowsy crowds of Harlem's Bowery, Lenox Avenue.

They made their way to the Lafayette, the Jew's gift of entertainment to Harlem colored folk. Each week the management of this theater presents a new musical revue of the three-a-day variety with motion pictures—all guaranteed to be from three to ten years old—sandwiched in between. On Friday nights there is a special midnight performance lasting from twelve o'clock until four or four-thirty the next morning, according to the stamina of the actors. The audience does not matter. It would as soon sit until noon the next day if the "high yaller" chorus girls would continue to tell stale jokes, just so long as there was a raucous blues singer thrown in every once in a while for vulgar variety.

Before Emma Lou and Alva could reach the entrance door, they had to struggle through a crowd of well-dressed young men and boys, congregated on the sidewalk in front of the theater. The midnight show at the Lafayette on Friday is quite a social event among certain classes of Harlem folk, and, if one is a sweet-

back or a man about town, one must be seen standing in front of
the theater, if not inside. It costs nothing to obstruct the entrance
way, and it adds much to one's prestige. Why, no one knows.

Without untoward incident Emma Lou and Alva found the
seats he had reserved. There was much noise in the theater,
much passing to and fro, much stumbling down dark aisles.
People were always leaving their seats, admonishing their companions to hold them, and some one was always taking them
despite the curt and sometimes belligerent, "This seat is taken."
Then, when the original occupant would return, there would be
still another argument. This happened so frequently that there
seemed to be a continual wrangling automatically staged in different parts of the auditorium. Then people were always looking
for some one or for something, always peering into the darkness,
emitting code whistles, and calling to Jane or Jim or Pete or Bill.
At the head of each aisle, both upstairs and down, people were
packed in a solid mass, a grumbling, garrulous mass, elbowing
their neighbors, cursing the management, and standing on tip-
toe trying to find an empty, intact seat—intact because every
other seat in the theater seemed to be broken. Hawkers went up
and down the aisle shouting, "Ice cream, peanuts, chewing gum,
or candy." People hissed at them and ordered what they wanted.
A sadly inadequate crew of ushers inefficiently led people up
one aisle and down another trying to find their supposedly
reserved seats; a lone fireman strove valiantly to keep the aisles
clear as the fire laws stipulated. It was a most chaotic and con-
fusing scene.

First, a movie was shown while the organ played mournful
jazz. About one o'clock the midnight revue went on. The curtain
went up on the customary chorus ensemble singing the customary, "Hello, we're glad to be here, we're glad to please you"
opening song. This was followed by the usual song-and-dance
team, a blues singer, a lady Charleston dancer, and two black-
faced comedians. Each would have his turn, then begin all over
again, aided frequently by the energetic and noisy chorus, which
somehow managed to appear upon the stage almost naked in
the first scene, and keep getting more and more naked as the
evening progressed.

Emma Lou had been to the Lafayette before with John and had been shocked by the scantily clad women and obscene skits. The only difference that she could see in this particular revue was that the performers were more bawdy and more boisterous. And she had never been in or seen such an audience. There was as much, if not more, activity in the orchestra and box seats than there was on the stage. It was hard to tell whether the cast was before or behind the proscenium arch. There seemed to be a veritable contest going on between the paid performers and their paying audience, and Emma Lou found the spontaneous monkey shines and utterances of those around her much more amusing than the stereotyped antic of the hired performers on stage.

She was surprised to find that she was actually enjoying herself, yet she supposed that after the house-rent party she could stand anything. Imagine people opening their flats to the public and charging any one who had the price to pay twenty-five cents to enter? Imagine people going to such bedlam Bacchanals?

A new scene on the stage attracted her attention. A very colorfully dressed group of people had gathered for a party. Emma Lou immediately noticed that all the men were dark, and that all the women were either a very light brown or "high yaller." She turned to Alva:

"Don't they ever have anything else but fair chorus girls?"

Alva made a pretense of being very occupied with the business on the stage. Happily, at that moment, one of a pair of black-faced comedians had set the audience in an uproar with a suggestive joke. After a moment Emma Lou found herself laughing, too. The two comedians were funny, no matter how prejudiced one might be against unoriginality. There must be other potent elements to humor besides surprise. Then a very Topsy-like girl skated onto the stage to the tune of "Ireland must be heaven because my mother came from there." Besides being corked until her skin was jet black, the girl had on a wig of kinky hair. Her lips were painted red—their thickness exaggerated by the paint. Her coming created a stir. Every one concerned was indignant that something like her should crash their party. She attempted to attach herself to certain men in the crowd. The straight men spurned her merely by turning away. The comedians made a great fuss about it, pushing her from one to the other, and finally getting into a riotous argument because each accused the other of having invited her. It ended by them agreeing to toss her bodily off the stage to the orchestral accompaniment of "Bye, Bye, Blackbird," while the entire party loudly proclaimed that "Black cats must go."

Then followed the usual rigamarole carried on weekly at the Lafayette concerning the undesirability of black girls. Every one, that is, all the males, let it be known that high browns and "high yallers" were "forty" with them, but that. . . . They were interrupted by the re-entry of the little black girl riding a mule and singing mournfully as she was being thus transported across the stage:

> A yellow gal rides in a limousine,
> A brown-skin rides a Ford,
> A black gal rides an old jackass
> But she gets there, yes, my Lord.

Emma Lou was burning up with indignation. So color-conscious had she become that any time some one mentioned or joked about skin color, she immediately imagined that they were referring to her. Now she even felt that all the people near by were looking at her and that their laughs were at her expense. She remained silent throughout the rest of the performance, averting her eyes from the stage and trying hard not to say anything to Alva before they left the theater. After what seemed an eternity, the finale screamed its good-bye at the audience, and Alva escorted her out into Seventh Avenue.

Alva was tired and thirsty. He had been up all night the night before at a party to which he had taken Geraldine, and he had had to get up unusually early on Friday morning in order to go after his laundry. Of course, when he arrived at Bobby's apartment where his laundry was being done, he found that his shirts were not yet ironed, so he had gone to bed there, with the result that he hadn't been able to go to sleep, nor had the shirts been ironed, but that was another matter.

"First time I ever went to a midnight show without some-

thing on my hip," he complained to Emma Lou as they crossed
the taxi-infested street in order to escape the crowds leaving
the theater and idling in front of it, even at four A.M. in the
morning.

"Well," Emma Lou returned vehemently, "it's the last time
I'll ever go to that place any kind of way."

Alva hadn't expected this. "What's the matter with you?"

"You're always taking me some place, or placing me in some
position where I'll be insulted."

"Insulted?" This was far beyond Alva. Who on earth had
insulted her and when. "But," he paused, then advanced cau-
tiously, "Sugar, I don't know what you mean."

Emma Lou was ready for a quarrel. In fact, she had been trying to pick one with him ever since the night she had gone to
that house-rent party, and the landlady had asked her to move
on the following day. Alva's curt refusal of her proposal that they
live together had hurt her far more than he had imagined.
Somehow or other he didn't think she could be so serious about
the matter, especially upon such short notice. But Emma Lou
had been so certain that he would be as excited over the suggestion as she had been that she hadn't considered meeting a definite refusal. Then the finding of a room had been irritating to
contemplate. She couldn't have called it irritating of accomplishment because Alva had done that for her. She had told him
on Sunday morning that she had to move and by Sunday night
he had found a place for her. She had to admit that he had
found an exceptionally nice place, too. It was just two blocks
from him, on 138th Street between Eighth Avenue and
Edgecombe. It was near the elevated station, near the park, and
cost only ten dollars and fifty cents per week for the room, kitchenette, and private bath.

On top of his refusing to live with her, Alva had broken two
dates with Emma Lou, claiming that he was playing poker. On
one of these nights, after leaving work, Emma Lou had decided
to walk past his house. Even at a distance she could see that
there was a light in his room, and when she finally passed the
house, she recognized Geraldine, the girl with whom she had
seen Alva dancing at the Renaissance Casino, seated in the

window. Angrily, she had gone home, determined to break with Alva on the morrow, and on reaching home had found a letter from her mother which had disturbed her even more. For a long time now her mother had been urging her to come home, and her Uncle Joe had even sent her word that he meant to forward a ticket at an early date. But Emma Lou had no intentions of going home. She was so obsessed with the idea that her mother didn't want her, and she was so incensed at the people with whom she knew she would be forced to associate, that she could consider her mother's hysterically put request only as an insult. Thus, presuming, she had answered in kind, giving vent to her feelings about the matter. This disturbing letter was in answer to her own spleenic epistle, and what hurt her most was, not the sharp counselings and verbose lamentations therein, but the concluding phrase, which read, "I don't see how the Lord could have given me such an evil, black hussy for a daughter."

The following morning she had telephoned Alva, determined to break with him, or at least make him believe she was about to break with him, but Alva had merely yawned and asked her not to be a goose. Could he help it if Braxton's girl chose to sit in his window? It was as much Braxton's room as it was his. True, Braxton wouldn't be there long, but while he was, he certainly should have full privileges. That had quieted Emma Lou then, but there was nothing that could quiet her now. She continued arguing as they walked toward 135th Street.

"You don't want to know what I mean."

"No, I guess not," Alva assented wearily, then quickened his pace. He didn't want to have a public scene with this black wench. But Emma Lou was not to be appeased.

"Well, you will know what I mean. First you take me out with a bunch of your supposedly high-toned friends, and sit silently by while they poke fun at me. Then you take me to a theater, where you know I'll have my feelings hurt." She stopped for breath. Alva filled in the gap.

"If you ask me," he said wearily, "I think you're full of stuff. Let's take a taxi. I'm too tired to walk." He hailed a taxi, pushed her into it, and gave the driver the address. Then he turned to

Emma Lou, saying something which he regretted having said a moment later.

"How did my friends insult you?"

"You know how they insulted me, sitting up there making fun of me 'cause I'm black."

Alva laughed, something he also regretted later.

"That's right, laugh, and I suppose you laughed with them then, behind my back, and planned all that talk before I arrived."

Alva didn't answer and Emma Lou cried all the rest of the way home. Once there he tried to soothe her.

"Come on Sugar, let Alva put you to bed."

But Emma Lou was not to be sugared so easily. She continued to cry. Alva sat down on the bed beside her.

"Snap out of it, won't you, Honey? You're just tired. Go to bed and get some sleep. You'll be all right tomorrow."

Emma Lou stopped her crying.

"I may be all right, but I'll never forget the way you've allowed me to be insulted in your presence."

This was beginning to get on Alva's nerves but he smiled at her indulgently:

"I suppose I should have gone down on the stage and biffed one of the comedians in the jaw?"

"No," snapped Emma Lou, realizing she was being ridiculous, "but you could have stopped your friends from poking fun at me."

"But, Sugar," this was growing tiresome. "How can you say they were making fun of you. It's beyond me."

"It wasn't beyond you when it started. I bet you told them about me before I came in, told them I was black. . . ."

"Nonsense, weren't some of them dark? I'm afraid," he advanced slowly, "that you are a trifle too color-conscious," he was glad he remembered that phrase.

Emma Lou flared up: "Color-conscious . . . who wouldn't be color conscious when everywhere you go people are always talking about color. If it didn't make any difference they wouldn't talk about it, they wouldn't always be poking fun, and laughing and making jokes. . . ."

Alva interrupted her tirade. "You're being silly, Emma Lou. About three-quarters of the people at the Lafayette tonight were either dark brown or black, and here you are crying and fuming like a ninny over some reference made on the stage to a black person." He was disgusted now. He got up from the bed. Emma Lou looked up.

"But, Alva, you don't know."

"I do know," he spoke sharply for the first time, "that you're a damn fool. It's always color, color, color. If I speak to any of my friends on the street you always make some reference to their color and keep plaguing me with—'Don't you know nothing else but light-skinned people?' And you're always beefing about being black. Seems like to me you'd be proud of it. You're not the only black person in this world. There are gangs of them right here in Harlem, and I don't see them going around a-moanin' 'cause they ain't half white."

"I'm not moaning."

"Oh, yes you are. And a person like you is far worse than a hinkty yellow nigger. It's your kind helps make other people color-prejudiced."

"That's just what I'm saying; it's because of my color. . . ."

"Oh, go to hell!" And Alva rushed out of the room, slamming the door behind him.

Braxton had been gone a week. Alva, who had been out with Marie, the creole Lesbian, came home late, and, turning on the light, found Geraldine asleep in his bed. He was so surprised that he could do nothing for a moment but stand in the center of the room and look—first at Geraldine and then at her toilet articles spread over his dresser. He twisted his lips in a wry smile, muttered something to himself, then walked over to the bed and shook her.

"Geraldine, Geraldine," he called. She awoke quickly and smiled at him.

"Hello. What time is it?"

"Oh," he returned guardedly, "somewhere after three."

"Where've you been?"

"Playing poker."

"With whom?"

"Oh, the same gang. But what's the idea?"

Geraldine wrinkled her brow.

"The idea of what?"

"Of sorta taking possession?"

"Oh," she seemed enlightened, "I've moved to New York."

It was Alva's cue to register surprise.

"What's the matter? You and your old lady fall out?"

"Not at all."

"Does she know where you are?"

"She knows I'm in New York."

"You know what I mean. Does she know you're going to stay?"

"Certainly."

"But where are you going to live?"

"Here."

"Here?"

"Yes."

"But . . . but . . . well, what is this all about, anyhow?"

She sat up in the bed and regarded him for a moment, a light smile playing around her lips. Before she spoke she yawned; then in a cool, even tone of voice, announced, "I'm going to have a baby."

"But," he began after a moment, "can't you—can't you . . . ?"

"I've tried everything and now it's too late. There's nothing to do but have it."

Part 5

Pyrrhic Victory

It was two years later. "Cabaret Gal," which had been on the road for one year, had returned to New York and the company had been disbanded. Arline was preparing to go to Europe and had decided not to take a maid with her. However, she determined to get Emma Lou another job before she left. She inquired among friends, but none of the active performers she knew seemed to be in the market for help, and it was only on the eve of sailing that she was able to place Emma Lou with Clere Sloane, a former stage beauty who had married a famous American writer and retired from public life.

Emma Lou soon learned to like her new place. She was Clere's personal maid, and found it much less tiresome than being in the theater with Arline. Clere was less temperamental and less hurried. She led a rather leisurely life, and treated Emma Lou more as a companion than a servant. Clere's husband, Campbell Kitchen, was very congenial and kind, too, although Emma Lou, at first, seldom came into contact with him, for he and his wife practically led separate existences, meeting only at meals, or when they had guests, or when they both happened to arise at the same hour for breakfast. Occasionally, they attended the theater or a party together, and sometimes entertained, but usually they followed their own individual paths.

Campbell Kitchen, like many other white artists and intellectuals, had become interested in Harlem. The Negro and all things negroid had become a fad, and Harlem had become a shrine to which feverish pilgrimages were in order. Campbell Kitchen, along with Carl Van Vechten, was one of the leading spirits in this "Explore Harlem; Know the Negro" crusade. He, unlike many others, was quite sincere in his desire to exploit those things in Negro life which he presumed would eventually win for the Negro a more comfortable position in American life. It was he who first began the agitation in the higher places of journalism which gave impetus to the spiritual craze. It was he who ferreted out and gave publicity to many unknown blues singers. It was he who sponsored most of the younger Negro writers, personally carrying their work to publishers and editors. It wasn't his fault entirely that most of them were published before they had anything to say or before they knew how to say it. Rather it was the fault of the faddistic American public which followed the band wagon and kept clamoring for additional performances, not because of manifested excellence, but rather because of their sensationalism and pseudo-barbaric *decor*.

Emma Lou had heard much of his activity, and had been surprised to find herself in his household. Recently he had written a book concerning Negro life in Harlem, a book calculated by its author to be a sincere presentation of those aspects of life in Harlem which had interested him. Campbell Kitchen belonged to the sophisticated school of modern American writers. His novels were more or less fantastic bits of realism, skipping lightly over the surfaces of life, and managing somehow to mirror depths through superficialities. His novel on Harlem had been a literary failure because the author presumed that its subject matter demanded serious treatment. Hence, he disregarded the traditions he had set up for himself in his other works, and produced an energetic and entertaining hodgepodge, where the bizarre was strangled by the sentimental, and the erotic clashed with the commonplace.

Negroes had not liked Campbell Kitchen's delineation of their life in the world's greatest colored city. They contended that, like "Nigger Heaven" by Carl Van Vechten, the book gave white people a wrong impression of Negroes, thus lessening their prospects of doing away with prejudice and race discrimination. From what she had heard, Emma Lou had expected to meet a sneering, obscene cynic, intent upon ravaging every Negro woman and insulting every Negro man, but he proved to be such an ordinary, harmless individual that she was won over to his side almost immediately.

Whenever they happened to meet, he would talk to her about her life in particular and Negro life in general. She had to admit that he knew much more about such matters than she or any other Negro she had ever met. And it was because of one of these chance talks that she finally decided to follow Mrs. Blake's advice and take the public school teachers' examination.

Two years had wrought little change in Emma Lou, although much had happened to her. After that tearful night, when Alva had sworn at her and stalked out of her room, she had somewhat taken stock of herself. She wondered if Alva had been right in his allegations. Was she supersensitive about her color? Did she encourage color prejudice among her own people, simply by being so expectant of it? She tried hard to place the blame on herself, but she couldn't seem to do it. She knew she hadn't been color-conscious during her early childhood days; that is, until she had had it called to her attention by her mother or some of her mother's friends, who had all seemed to take delight in marveling, "What an extraordinarily black child!" or "Such beautiful hair on such a black baby!"

Her mother had even hidden her away on occasions when she was to have company, and her grandmother had been cruel in always assailing Emma Lou's father, whose only crime seemed to be that he had had a blue black skin. Then there had been her childhood days when she had ventured forth into the streets to play. All of her colored playmates had been mulattoes, and her white playmates had never ceased calling public attention to her crow-like complexion. Consequently, she had grown sensitive and had soon been driven to play by herself, avoiding contact with other children as much as possible. Her mother encouraged her in this, had even suggested that she not attend certain parties because she might not have a good time.

Then there had been the searing psychological effect of that dreadful graduation night, and the lonely and embittering three years at college, all of which had tended to make her color more and more a paramount issue and ill. It was neither fashionable nor good for a girl to be as dark as she, and to be, at the same time, as untalented and undistinguished. Dark girls could get along if they were exceptionally talented or handsome or wealthy, but she had nothing to recommend her, save a beautiful head of hair. Despite the fact that she had managed to lead her classes in school, she had to admit that mentally she was merely mediocre and average. Now, had she been as intelligent as Mamie Olds Bates, head of a Negro school in Florida, and president of a huge national association of colored women's clubs, her darkness would not have mattered. Or had she been as wealthy as Lillian Saunders, who had inherited the millions her mother had made producing hair straightening commodities, things might have been different; but here she was, commonplace and poor, ugly and undistinguished.

Emma Lou recalled all these things, while trying to fasten the blame for her extreme color-consciousness on herself as Alva had done, but she was unable to make a good case of it. Surely, it had not been her color-consciousness which had excluded her from the only Negro sorority in her college, nor had it been her color-consciousness that had caused her to spend such an isolated three years in Southern California. The people she naturally felt at home with had, somehow or other, managed to keep her at a distance. It was no fun going to social affairs and being neglected throughout the entire evening. There was no need in forcing one's self into a certain milieu only to be frozen out. Hence, she had stayed to herself, had had very few friends, and had become more and more resentful of her blackness of skin.

She had thought Harlem would be different, but things had seemed against her from the beginning, and she had continued to go down, down, down, until she had little respect left for herself.

She had been glad when the road show of "Cabaret Gal" had gone into the provinces. Maybe a year of travel would set her aright. She would return to Harlem with considerable money saved, move into the Y.W.C.A., try to obtain a more congenial position, and set about becoming respectable once more, set about coming into contact with the "right sort of people." She was certain that there were many colored boys and girls in Harlem with whom she could associate and become content. She didn't wish to chance herself again with a Jasper Crane or an Alva.

Yet, she still loved Alva, no matter how much she regretted it, loved him enough to keep trying to win him back, even after his disgust had driven him away from her. She sadly recalled how she had telephoned him repeatedly, and how he had hung up the receiver with the brief, cruel "I don't care to talk to you," and she recalled how, swallowing her pride, she had gone to his house the day before she left New York. Alva had greeted her coolly, then politely informed her that he couldn't let her in, as he had other company.

This had made her ill, and for three days after "Cabaret Gal" opened in Philadelphia, she had confined herself to her hotel room and cried hysterically. When it was all over, she had felt much better. The outlet of tears had been good for her, but she had never ceased to long for Alva. He had been the only completely satisfying thing in her life, and it didn't seem possible for one who had pretended to love her as much as he, suddenly to become so completely indifferent. She measured everything by her own moods and reactions, translated everything into the language of Emma Lou, and variations bewildered her to the extent that she could not believe in their reality.

So, when the company had passed through New York on its way from Philadelphia to Boston, she had approached Alva's door once more. It had never occurred to her that any one save Alva would answer her knock, and the sight of Geraldine in a negligee had stunned her. She had hastened to apologize for knocking on the wrong door, and had turned completely away without asking for Alva, only to halt as if thunderstruck when she heard his voice, as Geraldine was closing the door, asking, "Who was it, Sugar?"

For a while, Alva had been content. He really loved Geraldine, or so he thought. To him she seemed eminently desirable in every respect, and now that she was about to bear him a child, well . . . he didn't yet know what they would do with it, but

everything would work out as it should. He didn't even mind
having to return to work nor, for the moment, mind having to
give less attention to the rest of his harem.

Of course, Geraldine's attachment of herself to him ruled
Emma Lou out more definitely than it did any of his other "paying off" people. He had been thoroughly disgusted with her and
had intended to relent only after she had been forced to chase
him for a considerable length of time. But Geraldine's coming
had changed things altogether. Alva knew when not to attempt
something, and he knew very well that he could not toy with
Emma Lou and live with Geraldine at the same time. Some of
the others were different. He could explain Geraldine to them,
and they would help him keep themselves secreted from her.
But Emma Lou, never! She would be certain to take it all
wrong.

The months passed; the baby was born. Both of the parents
were bitterly disappointed by this sickly, little "ball of tainted
suet," as Alva called it. It had a shrunken left arm and a deformed
left foot. The doctor ordered oil massages. There was a chance
that the infant's limbs could be shaped into some semblance of
normality. Alva declared that it looked like an idiot. Geraldine
had a struggle with herself, trying to keep from smothering it.
She couldn't see why such a monstrosity should live. Perhaps as
the years passed it would change. At any rate, she had lost her
respect for Alva. There was no denying to her that had she
mated with some one else, she might have given birth to a normal child. The pain she had experienced had shaken her. One
sight of the baby and continual living with it and Alva in that
one, now frowsy and odoriferous room, had completed her disil-
lusionment. For one of the very few times in her life, she felt
like doing something drastic.

Alva hardly ever came home. He had quit work once more
and started running about as before, only he didn't tell her
about it. He lied to her or else ignored her altogether. The baby
now a year old was assuredly an idiot. It neither talked nor
walked. Its head had grown out of all proportion to its body, and
Geraldine felt that she could have stood its shriveled arm and
deformed foot had it not been for its insanely large and vacant

eyes, which seemed never to close, and for the thick grinning lips, which always remained half open and through which came no translatable sounds.

Geraldine's mother was a pious woman, and, of course, denounced the parents for the condition of the child. Had they not lived in sin, this would not be. Had they married and lived respectably, God would not have punished them in this manner. According to her, the mere possession of a marriage license and an official religious sanction of their mating would have assured them a bouncing, healthy, normal child. She refused to take the infant. Her pastor advised her not to, saying that the parents should be made to bear the burden they had brought upon themselves.

For once, neither Geraldine nor Alva knew what to do. They couldn't keep on as they were now. Alva was drinking more and more. He was also becoming less interested in looking well. He didn't bother about his clothes as much as before, his almond-shaped eyes became more narrow, and the gray parchment conquered the yellow in his skin and gave him a death-like pallor. He hated that silent, staring idiot infant of his, and he had begun to hate its mother. He couldn't go into the room sober. Yet his drinking provided no escape. And though he was often tempted, he felt that he could not run away and leave Geraldine alone with the baby.

Then he began to need money. Geraldine couldn't work because some one had to look after the child. Alva wouldn't work now, and made no effort to come into contact with new "paying off" people. The old ones were not as numerous or as generous as formerly. Those who hadn't drifted away didn't care enough about the Alva of today to help support him, his wife, and child. Luckily, though, about this time, he "hit" the numbers twice in one month, and both he and Geraldine borrowed some money on their insurance policies. They accrued almost a thousand dollars from these sources, but that wouldn't last forever, and the problem of what they were going to do with the child still remained unsolved.

Both wanted to kill it, and neither had the courage to mention the word "murder" to the other. Had they been able to discuss this thing frankly with one another, they could have seen to it that the child smothered itself or fell from the crib sometime during the night. No one would have questioned the accidental death of an idiot child. But they did not trust one another, and neither dared to do the deed alone. Then Geraldine became obsessed with the fear that Alva was planning to run away from her. She knew what this would mean and she had no idea of letting him do it. She realized that should she be left alone with the child it would mean that she would be burdened throughout the years it lived, forced to struggle and support herself and her charge. But were she to leave Alva, some more sensible plan would undoubtedly present itself. No one expected a father to tie himself to an infant, and if that infant happened to be ill and an idiot . . . well, there were any number of social agencies which would care for it. Assuredly, she must get away first. But where to go?

She was stumped again and forced to linger, fearing all the while that Alva would fail to return home once he left. She tried desperately to reintroduce a note of intimacy into their relationship, tried repeatedly to make herself less repellent to him, and, at the same time, discipline her own self so that she would not communicate her apprehensions to him. She hired the little girl who lived in the next room to take charge of the child, bought it a store of toys, and went out to find a job. This being done, she insisted that Alva begin taking her out once again. He acquiesced. He wasn't interested one way or the other as long as he could go to bed drunk every night and keep a bottle of gin by his bedside.

Neither, though, seemed interested in what they were doing. Both were feverishly apprehensive at all times. They quarreled frequently, but would hasten to make amends to one another, so afraid were they that the first one to become angry might make a bolt for freedom. Alva drank more and more. Geraldine worked, saved, and schemed, always planning and praying that she would be able to get away first.

Then Alva was taken ill. His liquor-burned stomach refused to retain food. The doctor ordered him not to drink any more bootleg beverages. Alva shrugged his shoulders, left the doctor's office, and sought out his favorite speakeasy.

Emma Lou was busy, and being busy, had less time to think about herself than ever before. Thus, she was less distraught and much less dissatisfied with herself and with life. She was taking some courses in education in the afternoon classes at City College, preparatory to taking the next public school teacher's examination. She still had her position in the household of Campbell Kitchen, a position she had begun to enjoy and appreciate more and more as the master of the house evinced an interest in her and became her counselor and friend. He encouraged her to read and opened his library to her. Ofttimes he gave her tickets to musical concerts or to the theater, and suggested means of meeting what she called "the right sort of people."

She had moved meanwhile into the Y.W.C.A. There she had met many young girls like herself, alone and unattached in New York, and she had soon found herself moving in a different world altogether. She even had a pal, Gwendolyn Johnson, a likable, light-brown-skinned girl who had the room next to hers. Gwendolyn had been in New York only a few months. She had just recently graduated from Howard University, and was also planning to teach school in New York City. She and Emma Lou became fast friends and went everywhere together. It was with Gwendolyn that Emma Lou shared the tickets Campbell Kitchen gave her. Then on Sundays they would attend church. At first they attended a different church every Sunday, but finally took to attending St. Mark's A.M.E. Church on St. Nicholas Avenue regularly.

This was one of the largest and most high-toned churches in Harlem. Emma Lou liked to go there, and both she and Gwendolyn enjoyed sitting in the congregation, observing the fine clothes and triumphal entries of its members. Then, too, they soon became interested in the various organizations which the church sponsored for young people. They attended the meetings of a literary society every Thursday evening, and joined the young people's bible class which met every Tuesday evening. In this way, they came into contact with many young folk, and were often invited to parties and dances.

Gwendolyn helped Emma Lou with her courses in education

and the two obtained and studied copies of questions which had
been asked in previous examinations. Gwendolyn sympathized
with Emma Lou's color hypersensitivity and tried hard to make
her forget it. In order to gain her point, she thought it necessary
to put down light people, and with this in mind, ofttimes told
Emma Lou many derogatory tales about the mulattoes in the
social and scholastic life at Howard University in Washington,
D.C. The color question had never been of much moment to
Gwendolyn. Being the color she was, she had never suffered. In
Charleston, the mulattoes had their own church and their own
social life and mingled with the darker Negroes only when the
jim crow law or racial discrimination left them no other alternative. Gwendolyn's mother had belonged to one of these "persons of color" families, but she hadn't seen much in it at all.
What if she was better than the little black girl who lived around
the corner? Didn't they both have to attend the same colored
school, and didn't they both have to ride in the same section of
the street car, and were not they both subject to be called nigger
by the poor white trash who lived in the adjacent block?

She had thought her relatives and associates all a little silly
especially when they had objected to her marrying a man just
two or three shades darker than herself. She felt that this was
carrying things too far even in ancient Charleston, where cus-
toms, houses, and people all seemed antique and far removed
from the present. Stubbornly she had married the man of her
choice, and had exulted when her daughter had been nearer the
richer color of her father than the washed-out color of herself.
Gwendolyn's father had died while she was in college, and her
mother had begun teaching in a South Carolina Negro indus-
trial school, but she insisted that Gwendolyn must finish her
education and seek her career in the North.

Gwendolyn's mother had always preached for complete toler-
ance in matters of skin color. So afraid was she that her daughter
would develop a "pink" complex that she willingly discouraged
her associating with light people and persistently encouraged
her to choose her friends from among the darker elements of
the race. And she insisted that Gwendolyn must marry a dark
brown man so that her children would be real Negroes. So thor-

oughly had this become inculcated into her, that Gwendolyn often snubbed light people, and invariably, in accordance with her mother's sermonizings, chose dark-skinned friends and beaux. Like her mother, Gwendolyn was very exercised over the matter of intra-racial segregation and attempted to combat it verbally as well as actively.

When she and Emma Lou began going around together, trying to find a church to attend regularly, she had immediately black-balled the Episcopal Church, for she knew that most of its members were "pinks," and despite the fact that a number of dark-skinned West Indians, former members of the Church of England, had forced their way in, Gwendolyn knew that the Episcopal Church in Harlem, as in most Negro communities, was dedicated primarily to the salvation of light-skinned Negroes.

But Gwendolyn was a poor psychologist. She didn't realize that Emma Lou was possessed of a perverse bitterness and that she idolized the one thing one would naturally expect her to hate. Gwendolyn was certain that Emma Lou hated "yaller" niggers as she called them. She didn't appreciate the fact that Emma Lou hated her own color and envied the more mellow complexions. Gwendolyn's continual damnation of "pinks" only irritated Emma Lou and made her more impatient with her own blackness, for, in damning them, Gwendolyn also enshrined them for Emma Lou, who wasn't the least bit anxious to be classified with persons who needed a champion.

However, for the time being, Emma Lou was more free than ever from tortuous periods of self-pity and hatred. In her present field of activity, the question of color seldom introduced itself except as Gwendolyn introduced it, which she did continually, even to the extent of giving lectures on race purity and the superiority of unmixed racial types. Emma Lou would listen attentively, but all the while she was observing Gwendolyn's light-brown skin, and wishing to herself that it were possible for her and Gwendolyn to effect a change in complexions, since Gwendolyn considered a black skin so desirable.

They both had beaux, young men whom they had met at the various church meetings and socials. Gwendolyn insisted that

they snub the "high yallers" and continually was going into
ecstasies over the browns and blacks they conquested. Emma
Lou couldn't get excited over any of them. They all seemed so
young and pallid. Their air of being all-wise amused her, their
affected church purity and wholesomeness, largely a verbal matter, tired her. Their world was so small—church, school, home,
mother, father, parties, future. She invariably compared them to
Alva and made herself laugh by classifying them as a litter of sick
puppies. Alva was a bulldog and a healthy one at that. Yet these
sick puppies, as she called them, were the next generation of
Negro leaders, the next generation of respectable society folk.
They had a future; Alva merely lived for no purpose whatsoever
except for the pleasure he could squeeze out of each living
moment. He didn't construct anything; the litter of pups would.
or at least they would be credited with constructing something
whether they did or not. She found herself strangely uninterested in anything they might construct. She didn't see that it
would make much difference in the world whether they did or
did not. Months of sophisticated reading under Campbell
Kitchen's tutelage had cultivated the seeds of pessimism experience had sown. Life was all a bad dream recurrent in essentials.
Every dog had his day and every dog died. These priggish little
respectable persons she now knew and associated with seemed
infinitely inferior to her. They were all hypocritical and colorless. The committed what they called sin in the same colorless
way they served God, family, and race. None of them had the
fire or gusto of Alva, nor his light-heartedness. At last she had
met the "right sort of people" and found them to be quite
wrong.

However, she quelled her growing dissatisfaction and
immersed herself in her work. Campbell Kitchen had told her
again and again that economic independence was the solution to
almost any problem. When she found herself a well-paying position she need not worry more. Everything else would follow and
she would find herself among the pursued instead of among the
pursuers. This was the gospel she now adhered to and placed
faith in. She studied hard, finished her courses at Teachers
College, took and passed the school board examination, and

mechanically followed Gwendolyn about, pretending to share her enthusiasms and hatreds. All would soon come to the desired end. Her doctrine of pessimism was weakened by the optimism the future seemed to promise. She had even become somewhat interested in one of the young men she had met at St. Mark's. Gwendolyn discouraged this interest. "Why, Emma Lou, he's one of them yaller niggers; you don't want to get mixed up with him."

Though meaning well, she did not know that it was precisely because he was one of those "yaller niggers" that Emma Lou liked him.

Emma Lou and her new "yaller nigger," Benson Brown, were returning from church on a Tuesday evening where they had attended a young people's bible class. It was a beautiful early fall night, warm and moonlit, and they had left the church early, intent upon slipping away from Gwendolyn, and taking a walk before they parted for the night. Emma Lou had no reason for liking Benson save that she was flattered that a man as light as he should find himself attracted to her. It always gave her a thrill to stroll into church or down Seventh Avenue with him. And she loved to show him off in the reception room of the Y.W.C.A. True, he was almost as colorless and uninteresting to her as the rest of the crowd with whom she now associated, but he had a fair skin and he didn't seem to mind her darkness. Then, it did her good to show Gwendolyn that she, Emma Lou, could get a yellow-skinned man. She always felt that the reason Gwendolyn insisted upon her going with a dark-skinned man was because she secretly considered it unlikely for her to get a light one.

Benson was a negative personality. His father was an ex-preacher turned Pullman porter because, since prohibition times, he could make more money on the Pullman cars than he could in the pulpit. His mother was an active church worker and club woman, "one of the pillars of the community," the current pastor at their church had called her. Benson himself was in college, studying business methods and administration. It had taken him six years to finish high school, and it promised to take him much longer to finish college. He had a placid, ineffectual

dirty yellow face, topped by red mariney hair, and studded with
gray eyes. He was as ugly as he was stupid, and he had been as
glad to have Emma Lou interested in him as she had been glad
to attract him. She actually seemed to take him seriously, while
every one else more or less laughed at him. Already he was planning to quit school, go to work, and marry her; and Emma Lou,
while not anticipating any such sudden consummation, remained
blind to everything save his color and the attention he paid to
her.

Benson had suggested their walk and Emma Lou had chosen
Seventh Avenue in preference to some of the more quiet side
streets. She still loved to promenade up and down Harlem's
main thoroughfare. As usual on a warm night, it was crowded.
Street speakers and their audiences monopolized the corners.
Pedestrians and loiterers monopolized all of the remaining sidewalk space. The street was jammed with traffic. Emma Lou was
more convinced than ever that there was nothing like it anywhere. She tried to formulate some of her impressions and
attempted to convey them to Benson, but he couldn't see anything unusual or novel or interesting in a "lot of niggers hanging
out here to be seen." Then, Seventh Avenue wasn't so much.
What about Broadway or Fifth Avenue downtown where the
white folks gathered and strolled. Now those were the streets,
Seventh Avenue, Harlem's Seventh Avenue, didn't enter into
it.

Emma Lou didn't feel like arguing. She walked along in
silence, holding tightly to Benson's arm and wondering whether
or not Alva was somewhere on Seventh Avenue. Strange she had
never seen him. Perhaps he had gone away. Benson wished to
stop in order to listen to one of the street speakers who, he
informed Emma Lou, was mighty smart. It seemed that he was
the self-styled mayor of Harlem, and his spiel nightly was concerning the fact that Harlem Negroes depended upon white
people for most of their commodities instead of opening food
and dress commissaries of their own. He lamented the fact that
there were no Negro store owners, and regretted wealthy
Negroes did not invest their money in first-class butcher shops,
grocery stores, et cetera. Then, he perorated, the Jews, who now

grew rich off their Negro trade, would be forced out, and the money Negroes spent would benefit Negroes alone.

Emma Lou knew that this was just the sort of thing that Benson liked to hear. She had to tug hard on his arm to make him remain on the edge of the crowd, so that she could see the passing crowds rather than center her attention on the speaker. In watching, Emma Lou saw a familiar figure approach, a very trim, well-garbed figure, alert and swaggering. It was Braxton. She didn't know whether to speak to him or not. She wasn't sure that he would acknowledge her salute should she address him, yet here was her chance to get news of Alva, and she felt that she might risk being snubbed. It would be worth it. He drew near. He was alone, and, as he passed, she reached out her arm and touched him on the sleeve. He stopped, looked down at her and frowned.

"Braxton," she spoke quickly, "pardon me for stopping you, but I thought you might tell me where Alva is."

"I guess he's at the same place," he answered curtly, then moved away. Emma Lou bowed her head shamefacedly as Benson turned toward her long enough to ask who it was she had spoken to. She mumbled something about an old friend, then suggested they go home. She was tired. Benson agreed reluctantly and they turned toward the Y.W.C.A.

A taxi driver had brought Alva home from a saloon where he had collapsed from cramps in the stomach. That had been on Monday. The doctor had come and diagnosed his case. He was in a serious condition, his stomach lining was practically eaten away and his entire body wrecked from physical excess. Unless he took a complete rest and abstained from drinking liquor and all other forms of dissipation, there could be no hope of recovery. This hadn't worried Alva very much. He chafed at having to remain in bed, but possibility of death didn't worry him. Life owed him very little, he told Geraldine. He was content to let the devil take his due. But Geraldine was quite worried about the whole matter. Should Alva die or even be an invalid for any lengthy period, it would mean that she alone would have the burden of their misshapen child. She didn't want that burden.

In fact, she was determined not to have it. And neither did she intend to nurse Alva.

On the Friday morning after the Monday Alva had been taken ill, Geraldine had left for work as was her custom. But she did not come back that night. Every morning during that week she had taken away a bundle of this and a bundle of that until she had managed to get away most of her clothes. She had saved enough of her earnings to pay her fare to Chicago. She had chosen Chicago because a man who was interested in her lived there. She had written to him. He had been glad to hear from her. He ran a buffet flat. He needed some one like her to act as hostess. Leaving her little bundles at a girl friend's day after day and packing them away in a secondhand trunk, she had planned to leave the moment she received her pay on Saturday. She had intended going home on Friday night, but at the last moment she had faltered and reasoned that as long as she was away and only had twenty-four hours more in New York she might as well make her disappearance then. If she went back she might betray herself or else become soft-hearted and remain.

Alva was not very surprised when she failed to return home from work that Friday. The woman in the next room kept coming in at fifteen-minute intervals after five-thirty inquiring: "Hasn't your wife come in yet?" She wanted to get rid of the child which was left in her care daily. She had her own work to do, her own husband and child's dinner to prepare; and, furthermore, she wasn't being paid to keep the child both day and night. People shouldn't have children unless they intended taking care of them. Finally Alva told her to bring the baby back to his room . . . his wife would be in soon. But he knew full well that Geraldine was not coming back. Hell of a mess. He was unable to work, would probably have to remain in bed another week, perhaps two. His money was about gone, and now Geraldine was not there to pay the rent out of her earnings. Damn. What to do . . . what to do? He couldn't keep the child. If he put it in a home they would expect him to contribute to its support. It was too bad that he didn't know some one to leave this child of his with as his mother had done in his case. He began to wish for a drink.

Hours passed. Finally the lady came into the room again to see if he or the baby wanted anything. She knew Geraldine had not come in yet. The partition between the two rooms was so thin that the people in one were privy to everything the people in the other did or said. Alva told her his wife must have gone to see her sick mother in Long Island. He asked her to take care of the baby for him. He would pay her for her extra trouble. The whole situation offered her much pleasure. She went away radiant, eager to tell the other lodgers in the house her version of what had happened.

Alva got up and paced the room. He felt that he could no longer remain flat on his back. His stomach ached, but it also craved for alcoholic stimulant. So did his brain and nervous system in general. Inadvertantly, in one of his trips across the room, he looked into the dresser mirror. What he saw there halted his pacing. Surely that wan, dissipated, bloated face did not belong to him. Perhaps he needed a shave. He set about ridding himself of a week's growth of beard, but being shaved only made his face look more like the face of a corpse. It was liquor he needed. He wished to hell some one would come along and get him some. But no one came. He went back to bed, his eyes fixed on the clock, watching its hands approach midnight. Five minutes to go. . . . There was a knock on the door. Eagerly he sat up in the bed and shouted, "Come in."

But he was by no means expecting or prepared to see Emma Lou.

Emma Lou's room in the Y.W.C.A. at three o'clock that same morning. Emma Lou busy packing her clothes. Gwendolyn in negligee, hair disarrayed, eyes sleepy, yet angry:

"You mean you're going over there to live with that man?"

"Why not? I love him."

Gwendolyn stared hard at Emma Lou. "But don't you understand he's just tryin' to find some one to take care of that brat of his? Don't be silly, Emma Lou. He doesn't really care for you. If he did, he never would have deserted you as you once told me he did, or have subjected you to all those insults. And . . . he isn't your type of man. Why, he's nothing but a . . ."

"Will you mind tending to your own business, Gwendolyn,"
her purple powdered skin was streaked with tears.

"But what about your appointment?"

"I shall take it."

"What!" She forgot her weariness. "You mean to say you're
going to teach school and live with that man, too? Ain't you got
no regard for your reputation? I wouldn't ruin myself for no
yaller nigger. Here you're doing just what folks say a black gal
always does. Where is your intelligence and pride? I'm through
with you, Emma Lou. There's probably something in this stuff
about black people being different and more low than other
colored people. You're just a common ordinary nigger! God,
how I despise you!" And she rushed out of the room, leaving
Emma Lou dazed by the suddenness and wrath of her tirade.

Emma Lou was busier than she had ever been before in her
life. She had finally received her appointment and was teaching
in one of the public schools in Harlem. Doing this in addition to
nursing Alva and Alva Junior and keeping house for them in
Alva's same old room. Within six months she had managed to
make little Alva Junior take on some of the physical aspects of a
normal child. His little legs were in braces, being straightened.
Twice a week she took him to the clinic where he had violet ray
sun baths and oil massages. His little body had begun to fill out
and simultaneously it seemed as if his head was decreasing in
size. There was only one feature which remained unchanged;
his abnormally large eyes still retained their insane stare. They
appeared frozen and terrified as if their owner was gazing upon
some horrible yet fascinating object or occurrence. The doctor
said that this would disappear in time.

During those six months there had been a steady change in
Alva Senior, too. At first he had been as loving and kind to
Emma Lou as he had been during the first days of their relationship. Then, as he got better and began living his old life again,
he more and more relegated her to the position of a hired nurse
girl. He was scarcely civil to her. He seldom came home except
to eat and get some pocket change. When he did come home
nights, he was usually drunk, so drunk that his companions

would have to bring him home, and she would have to undress
him and put him to bed. Since his illness, he could not stand as
much liquor as before. His stomach refused to retain it, and his
legs refused to remain steady.

Emma Lou began to loathe him, yet ached for his physical
nearness. She was lonesome again, cooped up in that solitary
room with only Alva Junior for company. She had lost track of
all her old friends, and, despite her new field of endeavor, she
had made no intimate contacts. Her fellow colored teachers
were congenial enough, but they didn't seem any more inclined
to accept her socially than did her fellow white teachers. There
seemed to be some question about her antecedents. She didn't
belong to any of the collegiate groups around Harlem. She
didn't seem to be identified with any one who mattered. They
wondered how she had managed to get into the school system.

Of course Emma Lou made little effort to make friends
among them. She didn't know how. She was too shy to make an
approach and too suspicious to thaw out immediately when
some one approached her. The first thing she noticed was that
most of the colored teachers who taught in her school were
lighter colored than she. The darkest was a pleasing brown. And
she had noticed them putting their heads together when she
first came around. She imagined that they were discussing her.
And several times upon passing groups of them, she imagined
that she was being pointed out. In most cases what she thought
was true, but she was being discussed and pointed out not
because of her dark skin but because of the obvious traces of an
excess of rouge and powder which she insisted upon using.

It had been suggested, in a private council among the Negro
members of the teaching staff, that some one speak to Emma
Lou about this rather ludicrous habit of making up. But no one
had the nerve. She appeared so distant and so ready to take
offense at the slightest suggestion even of friendship that they
were wary of her. But after she began to be a standard joke
among the pupils and among the white teachers, they finally
decided to send her an anonymous note, suggesting that she use
fewer aids to the complexion. Emma Lou, on receiving the note,
at first thought that it was the work of some practical joker. It

never occurred to her that the note told the truth and that she looked twice as bad with paint and powder as she would without it. She interpreted it as being a means of making fun of her because she was darker than any one of the other colored girls. She grew more haughty, more acid, and more distant than ever. She never spoke to any one except as a matter of business. Then she discovered that her pupils had nicknamed her . . . "Blacker'n me."

What made her still more miserable was the gossip and comments of the woman in the next room. Lying in bed nights or else sitting at her table preparing her lesson plans, she could hear her telling every one who chanced in—

"You know that fellow in the next room? Well, let me tell you. His wife left him, yes-sireee, left him flat on his back in the bed, him and the baby, too. Yes, she did. Walked out of here just as big as you please to go to work one morning and she ain't come back yet. Then up comes this little black wench. I heard her when she knocked on the door that very night his wife left. At first he was mighty s'prised to see her and hugged her, a-tellin' her how much he loved her, and she crying like a fool all the time. I never heard the likes of it in my life. The next morning in she moves an' she's been here ever since. And you oughter see how she carries on over that child, just as loving, like as if she was his own mother. An' now that she's here an' workin' an' that nigger's well again, what does he do but go out an' get drunk worse than he uster with his wife. Would you believe it? Stays away three and four nights a week, while she hustles out of here an' makes time every morning. . . ."

On hearing this for about the twentieth time, Emma Lou determined to herself that she was not going to hear it again. (She had also planned to ask for a transfer to a new school, one on the east side in the Italian section where she would not have to associate with so many colored teachers.) Alva hadn't been home for four nights. She picked Alva Junior from out his crib and pulled off his nightgown, letting him lie naked in her lap. She loved to fondle his warm, mellow-colored body, loved to caress his little crooked limbs after the braces had been removed. She wondered what would become of him. Obviously she couldn't remain living with Alva, and she certainly couldn't keep Alva Junior forever. Suppose those evil school teachers should find out how she was living and report it to the school authorities? Was she morally fit to be teaching youth? She remembered her last conversation with Gwendolyn.

For the first time now she also saw how Alva had used her during both periods of their relationship. She also realized that she had been nothing more than a commercial proposition to him at all times. He didn't care for dark women either. He had never taken her among his friends, never given any signs to the public that she was his girl. And now when he came home with some of his boy friends, he always introduced her as Alva Junior's mammy. That's what she was, Alva Junior's mammy, and a typical black mammy at that.

Campbell Kitchen had told her that when she found economic independence, everything else would come. Well now that she had economic independence she found herself more enslaved and more miserable than ever. She wondered what he thought of her. She had never tried to get in touch with him since she had left the Y.W.C.A., and had never let him know of her whereabouts, had just quit communicating with him as unceremoniously as she had quit the Y.W.C.A. No doubt Gwendolyn had told him the whole sordid tale. She could never face him again unless she had made some effort to reclaim herself. Well, that's what she was going to do. Reclaim herself. She didn't care what became of Alva Junior. Let Alva and that yellow slut of a wife of his worry about their own piece of tainted suet.

She was leaving. She was going back to the Y.W.C.A., back to St. Mark's A.M.E. Church, back to Gwendolyn, back to Benson. She wouldn't stay here and have that child grow up to call her "black mammy." Just because she was black was no reason why she was going to let some yellow nigger use her. At once she was all activity. Putting Alva Junior's nightgown on, she laid him back into his crib and left him there crying while she packed her trunk and suitcase. Then, asking the woman in the next room to watch him until she returned, she put on her hat and coat and started for the Y.W.C.A., making plans for the future as she went.

Halfway there she decided to telephone Benson. It had been seven months now since she had seen him, seven months since, without a word of warning or without leaving a message, she had disappeared, telling only Gwendolyn where she was going. While waiting for the operator to establish connections, she recalled the conversation she and Gwendolyn had had at the time, recalled Gwendolyn's horror and disgust on hearing what Emma Lou planned doing, recalled . . . some one was answering the 'phone. She asked for Benson, and in a moment heard his familiar:

"Hello."

"Hello, Benson, this is Emma Lou." There was complete silence for a moment, then:

"Emma Lou?" he dinned into her ear. "Well, where have you been. Gwennie and I have been trying to find you."

This warmed her heart; coming back was not going to be so difficult after all.

"You did?"

"Why, yes. We wanted to invite you to our wedding."

The receiver fell from her hand. For a moment she stood like one stunned, unable to move. She could hear Benson on the other end of the wire clicking the receiver and shouting "Hello, Hello," then the final clicking of the receiver as he hung up, followed by a deadened . . . "operator" . . . "operator" from central. Somehow or other she managed to get hold of the receiver and replace it in the hook. Then she left the telephone booth and made her way out of the drugstore and into the street. Seventh Avenue as usual was alive and crowded. It was an early spring evening and far too warm for people to remain cooped up in stuffy apartments. Seventh Avenue was the gorge into which Harlem cliff dwellers crowded to promenade. It was heavy laden, full of life and color, vibrant and leisurely. But for the first time since her arrival in Harlem, Emma Lou was impervious to all this. For the moment she hardly realized where she was. Only the constant jostling and the raucous ensemble of street noises served to bring her out of her daze.

Gwendolyn and Benson married. "What do you want to

waste time with that yaller nigger for? I wouldn't marry a yaller nigger."

"Blacker'n me" . . . "Why don't you take a hint and stop plastering your face with so much rouge and powder."

Emma Lou stumbled down Seventh Avenue, not knowing where she was going. She noted that she was at 135th Street. It was easy to tell this particular corner. It was called the campus. All the college boys hung out there when the weather permitted, obstructing the traffic and eyeing the passersby professionally. She turned west on 135th Street. She wanted quiet. Seventh Avenue was too noisy and too alive and too happy. How could the world be happy when she felt like she did? There was no place for her in the world. She was too black, black is a portent of evil, black is a sign of bad luck.

> A yaller gal rides in a limousine
> A brown-skin does the same;
> A black gal rides in a rickety Ford,
> But she gets there, yes, my Lord.

"Alva Junior's black mammy." "Low down common nigger." "Jes' crazy 'bout that littler yaller brat."

She looked up and saw a Western Union office sign shining above a lighted doorway. For a moment she stood still, repeating over and over to herself Western Union, Western Union, as if to understand its meaning. People turned to stare at her as they passed. They even stopped and looked up into the air trying to see what was attracting her attention, and, seeing nothing, would shrug their shoulders and continue on their way. The Western Union sign suggested only one thing to Emma Lou and that was home. For the moment she was ready to rush into the office and send a wire to her Uncle Joe, asking for a ticket, and thus be able to escape the whole damn mess. But she immediately saw that going home would mean beginning her life all over again, mean flying from one degree of unhappiness into another probably much more intense and tragic than the present one. She had once fled to Los Angeles to escape Boise, then fled to Harlem to escape Los Angeles, but these mere geographical flights had not solved her problems in the past, and a

further flight back to where her life had begun, although facile
of accomplishment, was too futile to merit consideration.

Rationalizing thus, she moved away from in front of the
Western Union office and started toward the park two blocks
away. She felt that it was necessary that she do something about
herself and her life and do it immediately. Campbell Kitchen
had said that every one must find salvation within one's self, that
no one in life need be a total misfit, and that there was some
niche for every peg, whether that peg be round or square. If this
were true then surely she could find hers even at this late date.
But then hadn't she exhausted all possibilities? Hadn't she
explored every province of life and everywhere met the same
problem? It was easy for Campbell Kitchen or for Gwendolyn
to say what they would do had they been she, for they were looking at her problem in the abstract, while to her it was an empir-
ical reality. What could they know of the adjustment proceed-
ings necessary to make her life more full and more happy? What
could they know of her heartaches?

She trudged on, absolutely oblivious to the people she passed
or to the noise and bustle of the street. For the first time in her
life she felt that she must definitely come to some sort of conclusion about her life and govern herself accordingly. After all,
she wasn't the only black girl alive. There were thousands on
thousands who, like her, were plain, untalented, ordinary, and
who, unlike herself, seemed to live in some degree of comfort.
Was she alone to blame for her unhappiness? Although this had
been suggested to her by others, she had been too obtuse to
accept it. She had ever been eager to shift the entire blame on
others when no doubt she herself was the major criminal.

But having arrived at this—what did it solve or promise for
the future? After all, it was not the abstractions of her case
which at the present moment most needed elucidation. She
could strive for a change of mental attitudes later. What she
needed to do now was to accept her black skin as being real and
unchangeable, to realize that certain things were, had been, and
would be, and with this in mind begin life anew, always fighting,
not so much for acceptance by other people, but for acceptance

of herself by herself. In the future she would be eminently self-ish. If people came into her life—well and good. If they didn't—she would live anyway, seeking to find herself and achieving meanwhile economic and mental independence. Then possibly, as Campbell Kitchen had said, life would open up for her, for it seemed as if its doors yielded more easily to the casual, self-centered individual than to the ranting, praying pilgrim. After all, it was the end that mattered, and one only wasted time and strength seeking facile open-sesame means instead of pushing along a more difficult and direct path.

By now Emma Lou had reached St. Nicholas Avenue and was about to cross over into the park when she heard the chimes of a clock and was reminded of the hour. It was growing late—too late for her to wander in the park alone where she knew she would be approached either by some persistent male or an insulting park policeman. Wearily she started toward home, realizing that it was necessary for her to get some rest in order to be in her class room on the next morning. She mustn't jeop-ardize her job, for it was partially through the money she was earning from it that she would be able to find her place in life. She was tired of running up blind alleys all of which seemed to converge and lead her ultimately to the same blank wall. Her motto from now on would be "find—not seek." All things were at one's fingertips. Life was most kind to those who were judi-cious in their selections, and she, weakling that she now realized she was, had not been a connoisseur.

As she drew nearer home she felt certain that should she attempt to spend another night with Alva and his child, she would surely smother to death during the night. And even though she felt this, she also knew within herself that no matter how much at the present moment she pretended to hate Alva, that he had only to make the proper advances in order to win her to him again. Yet she also knew that she must leave him if she was to make her self-proposed adjustment—leave him now even if she should be weak enough to return at some not so distant date. She was determined to fight against Alva's influ-ence over her, fight even though she lost, for she reasoned that even in losing she would win a pyrrhic victory and thus make her life less difficult in the future, for having learned to fight future battles would be easy.

She tried to convince herself that it would not be necessary for her to have any more Jasper Cranes or Alvas in her life. To assure herself of this she intended to look John up on the morrow and if he were willing let him re-enter her life. It was clear to her now what a complete fool she had been. It was clear to her at last that she had exercised the same discrimination against her men and the people she wished for friends that they had exercised against her—and with less reason. It served her right that Jasper Crane had fooled her as he did. It served her right that Alva had used her once for the money she could give him and again as a black mammy for his child. That was the price she had had to pay for getting what she thought she wanted. But now she intended to balance things. Life after all was a give and take affair. Why should she give important things and receive nothing in return?

She was in front of the house now and looking up saw that all the lights in her room were lit. And as she climbed the stairs she could hear a drunken chorus of raucous masculine laughter. Alva had come home meanwhile, drunk of course and accompanied by the usual drunken crowd. Emma Lou started to turn back, to flee into the street—anywhere to escape being precipitated into another sordid situation, but remembering this was to be her last night there, and that the new day would find her beginning a new life, she subdued her flight impulse and without knocking threw open the door and walked into the room. She saw the usual and expected sight: Alva, face a death mask, sitting on the bed embracing an effeminate boy whom she knew as Bobbie, and who drew hurriedly away from Alva as he saw her. There were four other boys in the room, all in varied states of drunkenness—all laughing boisterously at some obscene witticism. Emma Lou suppressed a shudder and calmly said "Hello Alva"—The room grew silent. They all seemed shocked and surprised by her sudden appearance. Alva did not answer her greeting but instead turned to Bobbie and asked him for another drink. Bobbie fumbled nervously at his hip pocket and finally

produced a flask which he handed to Alva. Emma Lou stood at
the door and watched Alva drink the liquor Bobbie had given
him. Every one else in the room watched her. For the moment
she did not know what to say or what to do. Obviously she
couldn't continue standing there by the door nor could she leave
and let them feel she had been completely put to rout.

Alva handed the flask back to Bobbie, who got up from the
bed and said something about leaving. The others in the room
also got up and began staggering around looking for their hats.
Emma Lou thought for a moment that she was going to win
without any further struggle, but she had not reckoned with
Alva, who, meanwhile, had sufficiently emerged from his stupor
to realize that his friends were about to go.

"What the hell's the matter with you," he shouted up at
Bobbie, and without waiting for an answer reached out for
Bobbie's arm and jerked him back down on the bed.

"Now stay there till I tell you to get up."

The others in the room had now found their hats and started
toward the door, eager to escape. Emma Lou crossed the room
to where Alva was sitting and said, "You might make less noise,
the baby's asleep."

The four boys had by this time opened the door and staggered out into the hallway. Bobbie edged nervously away from
Alva, who leered up at Emma Lou and snarled, "If you don't like
it—"

For the moment Emma Lou did not know what to do. Her
first impulse was to strike him, but she was restrained because
underneath the loathsome beast that he now was, she saw the
Alva who had first attracted her to him, the Alva she had always
loved. She suddenly felt an immense compassion for him and
had difficulty in stifling an unwelcome urge to take him into her
arms. Tears came into her eyes, and for a moment it seemed as
if all her rationalization would go for naught. Then once more
she saw Alva, not as he had been, but as he was now, a drunken,
drooling libertine, struggling to keep the embarrassed Bobbie in
a vile embrace. Something snapped within her. The tears in her
eyes receded, her features grew set, and she felt herself harden-
ing inside. Then, without saying a word, she resolutely turned

away, went into the alcove, pulled her suitcases down from the shelf in the clothes-closet, and to the blasphemous accompaniment of Alva berating Bobbie for wishing to leave, finished packing her clothes, not stopping even when Alva Junior's cries deafened her, and caused the people in the next room to stir uneasily.